Missing The Laughter

Written & Published

By

Jude Gallagher Barnes

Front cover photo courtesy of Lillian Milsom from Studio Kathleen Kinnaird

Back cover photo courtesy of author's private collection

ISBN 978-0-6151-6584-4

For St. Jude

For
Keith,
Always

Contents

Preface

You must ask yourself one very important question: Why give up the drug and maintain the behavior? I suspect that we look to the drug of our choice; whether it is pills, alcohol, another person or even the behavior itself as the problem when it isn't. I suspect that the problem is the drama involved. The drug we use to access that emotional life is secondary to the fact that we subconsciously feel the need to be drawn into an emotional life. Once we know what draws us into the drama and our actual addiction to it – so much so that we willingly create it in our everyday lives via our "drug" of choice – then it loses its power over us.

What it really boils down to is simply growing up and taking responsibility for our actions and for our lives.

Imagine the many-splendored things that we miss because of the superfluous drama with which we fill our lives.

Think about it…

Acknowledgments

Friend ---
A person one knows, likes and trusts.
I would like for you to meet some of my friends…
Ann Marie
Carole
Ellen
Elaine
Jack
Jaime
Jim
Joanne
Josie
Judy
Justin
Kathy
Lillian
Linda
Lon
Lorie
Marlene
Mary
Pamela
Paul
Rose

Missing The Laughter

01-Jun-04

A man and his daughter are sitting in a restaurant in upper Manhattan. In the midst of an everyday conversation, he turns to her and says, "I miss the laughter." His daughter backtracks and focuses on what her father has just said. Leaning over to touch his hand, she asks, "Dad, what are you talking about?" He looks at her and sighs, "I miss the laughter Jim brought into my life."

This is an odd feeling, going back and revisiting all of this and documenting as I go. This is a simple story, a running commentary on one part of my life. What is the secret of life? If there is one, I'd have to say that my experiences have taught me to face every challenge head-on; fear nothing because it is put there to teach you something so that you can move on to the next phase of your life. If you ignore it, you're just spinning your wheels in shit. In other words, you are not living your life; you are not learning from what it has to offer, you exist, mark time. That is the secret...**LIVE** your life. The telling of this story is mainly for my benefit, alone. Believe me when I tell you that the power of the written word is compelling. Once writ, it is real. This is a journey for me into my past to try and alleviate some of the pressures of my present and bring hope for my future. As Pope John Paul II said about 'The Passion,' "It is as it was."

To be sure, this is going to hurt, but what in life worth having doesn't...ready...?

Chapter One

"Love walked right in and…"

I met Jackson during the week between Christmas and New Year's, 1988. A friend was in town for the holidays and we decided to go out for a drink, as we were both "single" and celebrating the coming new year alone. I can still remember sitting there talking with my friend Tom, but feeling that someone was staring at me and when I looked, there stood Jackson against the wall; tall, broad-shouldered, long, curly blonde hair, blue eyes, a brilliant smile, standing about 20 feet from me, staring and smiling, waiting for me to notice him. I noticed him and went back to my conversation...he wasn't going to give up that easily. He came closer, and then closer. Eventually, I asked my friend if he knew who the blonde was and Tom looked and said that he didn't, but apparently either that dumb blonde knew me or wanted to. So, I looked at Jackson, smiled and crooked my finger for him to come over, which he did. I introduced myself, asked him his name, and sent him away. He was totally confused, came back, and I told him that I wanted to know who was staring at me. He laughed and sat down, as it was getting crowded, and we talked briefly. He was with friends and they were going to another bar, but he asked if I would still be here in about an hour or so, and I told him I might and if so, we again could pick up our conversation. With that, he left with his friends and I thought nothing more of it, other than to comment to Tom on how these guys who were out to score made me laugh. You know the type. What I call, "Body by God, Brain by Mattel". So, Tom and I continued our conversation and drinking, and how men were all heels, who needed them (We did!!!), and I had a really good time, as I recall; however, Tom had to move on, heading to Wisconsin to visit family. I was actually gathering my things to leave when in walked Jackson, who made a beeline right for me so I'd sit back down. I admit it was a pleasant feeling having someone notice me. It had been a long time and I was thirsty for a man's attention.

We spent the rest of that night together talking (Yes, talking) and I gave him my phone number. I thought that would be the end of it. I did not think about it beyond that point. I believe that was a Sunday and I went back to my little apartment, back to my little job, back to my little life, thank you. Then the phone started ringing. It was Jackson. "How about going out for dinner?" "Nope, don't think I can do that." Next day...."How about a movie?" "Um, nope." Next night..."How about coming here for dinner?" "Busy, can't." This went on for over a week. I cancelled five dates in a row with this guy and still he wouldn't give up and call it a day. The phone calls. I would listen. I gave him what he wanted which was my undivided attention. I'm very good at doing that with a man. It's not that hard to do. They think it's incredible. You focus on their eyes, smile and nod once in a while, and they're in seventh heaven thinking you're all theirs when you're actually thinking about the dry cleaning you still haven't picked up, or when did you last clean the bathroom?? It was a trick I'd learned as a kid in having to deal with my alcoholic father. Focusing on him and letting him talk was good. The more he talked, the less chance there was of my getting a beating. Anyway, as it turned out, Jackson had to go to Georgia. Yep, good-looking AND southern. To Georgia, as his mother had passed away. Thinking about it later, I was struck by the fact that when he told me that his mother had died there wasn't a drop of emotion expressed, not one. Excuse me, this may not seem alien to some of you, but I'm Italian. When your mother dies, it's a big thing. What I mistook for inner strength was actually a stoicism that ran through him like a vein of cold, hard steel. Talk about a Steel Magnolia. Honey, Sherman would have retreated rather than deal with Jackson. His mother passed away and he was heading down there for the funeral...with...his...daughter. Daughter? Daughter. Hmm...Daughter. That meant there was a W.I.F.E. at some point in the picture. I had a diehard rule; never, under any circumstances, ever become involved with married men. No need to discuss it, it is self-explanatory. A dead-end street, my friend. Just a brick wall from which to peel your face after hitting. You know, that should have been my first clue. Did I follow my own rule? No one to blame, but moi.

To give you a little background, I was carrying some deep pain. I had been in a relationship for almost two years, only to have it turn out that he was mentally ill. Very wealthy, very "Rebecca", may I say. Because of some strange behavior on his part, I learned the truth, and the relationship was forced to come to an end. I thought it would kill me. I never totally walked away from that devastation. The first time I ever really knew love in my life. There are moments in life where you leave a part of yourself, an emotional marker of sorts. They become the stones in the path that becomes your life and they are washed clean with the tears you shed over them during the years. Now, six months later, I have this blonde hunk that can't take his eyes from me. ***WHO ARE YOU AND WHAT DO YOU WANT?*** I was quite content stewing in my misery. I didn't need someone coming in, trying to get my attention away from this train-wreck that had occurred in my life. I was content to sit there playing it over and over again in my mind doing the body count. The weight I'd lost in the process was incredible. I looked fabulous...But, Jackson wasn't about to let me stew in self-pity and remorse. He had other ideas.

Of course, I could take the easy route and blame my friend, Lee, who was dating Jackson's roommate at the time and kept calling and nagging me to "go out with the guy. He's really nice and you're all he talks about. One date and get it over with. He's driving us nuts wondering why you won't go out with him." I should have stuck with my gut instinct, but I didn't. I started feeling sorry for him. All the effort he was putting into this on the chance that I might go out with him was too much. I began chiding myself for being so conceited and arrogant because I failed to realize his feelings in all of this. Oh yea, I dragged myself down that road and finally caved. Out for dinner we went. Some Chinese place in Rochester. He claimed to know the owner. I said, "Good. You can tell him about the cockroach sitting next to me in the booth." Poor Jackson. I recall saying that a lot when we first met. Poor Jackson. Anyway, we finally had dinner and it actually went well. We laughed and talked and shared. He started opening up which was good and I sat back and let him have center stage that night. So, we finished and went back to his house and I don't really recall ever leaving. It was very strange. I'd never had that kind of relationship before. I'd be home and there was Jackson. I'd be at work and Jackson was on the phone. I'd be in a restaurant and in walked Jackson. Jackson would call me every day and want me to come over to his house for dinner, or to watch a movie, or to spend time with his daughter. I think today it's called stalking, but "in the day," it was flattering and overwhelming. That's basically what happened and how we got together. He wore me down. And still, my gut instinct was to walk away. What a fool I was not to read my own damn radar screen and see what was coming. I tried, but I just would not listen.

In the beginning, dating Jackson was a lot of fun. You could tell that he hadn't had a lot of experience in the dating scene, in general, with either men or women. Jackson was the ugly duckling who became a beautiful swan. I know because I was there for the ten-year transformation. It was fun watching someone take his first steps in a lifestyle which I had taken for granted most of my life, and for me was the "norm." I enjoyed showing him how to do it, how to live a gay lifestyle. I enjoyed overcoming obstacles with him so he wouldn't be hurt by society, as we had been, those of us who were born gay. "Living a gay lifestyle." All that really means is living your life as yourself, period. No advertising or flaunting. No need for tons of jewelry complete with limp wrist and swishing hips and a lighted cigarette being used as a pointer during a conversation. No back-alley Bette Davis diva. Just being you. It was easy to tell that Jackson had been the quiet one in school, the teacher's pet, the nerd, and because of it had been hurt. He had closed himself off and lived a life that society found acceptable so he could achieve what he had wanted to as a career path. I thought that was admirable, but terribly repressive. Your natural desires will always find an outlet so it's best to be yourself, instead of developing personality quirks in order to vent your true feelings. I wanted to show Jackson how to do this, if I could. I actually found myself liking him as a person and enjoying being in his company. He had this one flaw, though. Let me add something here that needs to be said. I very often find in gay men, who try and hide their true selves that "quirk". It's as if they are bent on society knowing the truth, one way or another. So, they have that swish, or wear too much jewelry, or have developed a sense of sarcasm, as a way of letting people if not know for sure, then wonder about, their sexual preference. The benefit to that I guess is that many end up wondering, but few actually have the courage to ask and therein lies your safety net. Jackson's quirk was that he had this voice, this way of speaking, which made you stop and look because it had absolutely nothing to do with what you were seeing in front of you. I used to tell people that it was as if the ghost of Marilyn Monroe was channeling through Jackson. He has this very soft, mid-to-upper-range voice, just like Marilyn's. The closest I can come to a comparison that's living would be Michael Jackson. I used to pray he'd catch a cold so his voice would deepen. It drove me nuts when Jackson would open his mouth. And, you'd see people's reactions. When we'd go to restaurants, I'd always end up saying, "I'll order." People today have no qualms with expressing their feelings, either by the way they look at you or how they treat you, based on what they are seeing and/or hearing. It doesn't matter how much money you have, as Jackson discovered, people will react to something that is obvious. And his "quirk" was very obvious. That thing that some gay men have of pronouncing every damn consonant in a word, spraying you with spit on that final "T" or, God help you if they come across a word with an "S" in it. Sorry, but subconsciously, they know how they sound and they look for that reaction. Okay, deal with what is thrown your way, kid. Don't stand there wondering why you're the brunt of the joke. People do not deal well with something that makes them feel uncomfortable. The majority wants to fit in; they want to be accepted. As they say today, "Deal with it." My mother always taught us, "What you do behind your own four walls is your business, but what you do outside of those four walls becomes the world's business." Now, isn't that the truth and a hard pill to swallow. I ignored his voice because I loved him, but maybe I was using him to let the world know that I was gay? The way I felt was that it came with the package and I loved the package.

I began looking at Jackson's other personal relationships; to see how he dealt with people he loved, in general. Not necessarily well is what I discovered. Jackson was recovering from a recent nervous breakdown, brought on by the pressures of his divorce. He and his ex-wife worked for the same company. Part of the divorce agreement had been that their private lives would not be discussed at the work place. Hmm…that's right. As soon as it went "With Pen in Hand," she told everyone at work why they had divorced, namely because of his homosexuality. As he wanted to work up the corporate ladder, he found that the pressure this brought to bare was too overwhelming. So, he snapped one day while at work. It was at this point in his life that we met. Jackson had gone back to work. Personally, I found it admirable that he could face these people again and I stood with him and helped support him through the next year which was particularly agonizing for him.

Jackson and his ex-wife were having a battle royal since their divorce papers had been filed and they had seen a court-appointed mediator, regarding their daughter. From what Jackson told me, his ex-wife was only interested in the money; how much support was coming…for how long, and his daughter was a pawn that they both used in this war they had going. It struck me that Jackson thrived on this sort of thing because it still made him a controlling part of his ex-wife's life. She seemed to enjoy the battle, sensing it kept her a part of his life. The games we play on and with one another. Personally, I never saw the point to it. I saw a child, much like myself at ten years of age, caught in the middle. Not knowing why her father left, or if she had been a part of that rejection. That you could see on her face. She was so emotionally insecure when I first met her and I identified immediately with that vulnerability in her. She was the kid whose nose was always running; who wore to school whatever was nearest in the morning, but not necessarily the cleanest outfit. She was the one with the stringy hair hanging in her eyes, etc. That was when I met her; a raw open nerve of emotion, confusion and heartache, but she loved to laugh. Well, so did I. Whatever time we spent together was high energy and loaded with laughter, usually at the expense of her father. Actually, our first meeting was not the best introduction.

I had been invited to Jackson's house for dinner and to meet his daughter. When I arrived, there was a lot of noise coming from the dining room. It was his daughter dancing on top of the dining room table. I walked in and stood there, watching, not saying anything. Finally, Jackson asked her to turn around so that he could introduce us. When he did, I asked her if this was how she usually met strangers. That sort of set the tone for the evening. I immediately showed her where I stood with her behavior and what I would accept. The dancing stopped. Jackson also had a cat by the name of "Shadow." A beautiful cat, but with free reign of the house. While we were having dinner, Shadow decided to jump up onto the tabletop and sniff at everyone's plate. My mother would have died. I sat there in silence as

Jackson was talking, and watched the cat get closer and closer to my plate. Finally, I said in the midst of Jackson's conversation, "Who taught your cat the Helen Keller routine?" Jackson fell out, laughing. Shadow was removed from the dining room. I sensed that evening that I was being tested and so I thought, "What the hell do I have to lose? I might as well let them know now how I feel about such things."

As for the rest of his family, when I first met Jackson, he was only associating with one of his sisters, Marilyn, who lived in South Carolina. Their connection was that he was sending her a check every month because she was so deep in debt, but she always seemed to spend his check on even more clothes, jewelry, etc., instead of paying down what she owed. Yet another woman in whose life Jackson was a controlling factor. All these very twisted and interwoven family relationships are what I was beginning to see. And, they were not good signs. So, enabler that I am, I started writing to his older sister Rachel and kept in touch with her when we moved, and she started calling her little brother, and before you knew it, voila. They were speaking again. That left his younger brother, Randall, whom he despised, and his father, Big Willy. Big Willy was raised on a farm in Alabama. Big Willy ended up marrying his first cousin when his wife passed on, the very same first cousin whom he'd been having an affair with since high school. I gather that since this was illegal in most states in the United States, Big Willy was discouraged from pursuing this familial relationship and told to go looking on the other side of the fence for a stranger to woo and marry. So, Big Willy did just that, landing Jackson's mother, a moneyed southern lady. However, that did not stop him from pursuing his affair with his first cousin despite the fact that she too had also married. I pitied Jackson's mother and thought that she probably found death to be a peaceful solution to the demons that haunted her during her married life. Jackson and Big Willy had not been close in many years. His brother, Randall, more or less usurped Jackson's position as the oldest son and therefore the favored son, as well, in his father's eyes. Of course, it was that voice thing too that I'd told you about earlier, about Jackson. His brother didn't carry that "trait." They hate one another. So be it. Cross that one off the list for Christmas. But, with time and conniving, Rachel and I were able to get Jackson to talk with Big Willy, as their father would spend time at Rachel's house in Macon on weekends, so we decided that would be a good time to call one another. Little by little it worked on Jackson, and eventually his father even began calling Rochester and actually came for a visit, with his first cousin, of course. They hadn't wed at that point, but they were very "well-traveled". My God, talk about Hooterville. These southerners can be too much. Here, I'm expecting the cousin to be wearing gloves with a bubble hairdo or something as outdated, and in walks this "thing" with the cigarette hanging from her mouth, dyed hair, jewelry (Of course), and mouth going a mile-a-minute. Meet the "cousin." Common trailer trash dripping in Diamonique. I never let Jackson live down that one, believe me. But, my point in all of this was to try and make Jackson see that they were still his family. No matter what he did with his life or where he may go with it, they were still his family. I'm sorry to beat a dead horse here, but to an Italian, "La Familia" can be everything. So, we were going to work this through and get beyond it, somehow. One relative at a time if need be, minus the "cousin," that fleabag from Mobile.

Chapter Two

"Yours, Mine & Ours"

Easter was approaching and I had asked my mother to come up from Pennsylvania to spend the holiday with me. As a couple of months had gone by, I also wanted her to meet Jackson and his daughter. I knew that his daughter would cling to her. Her maternal grandmother lived in Florida and they were NOT close, and as the story began, she went to Georgia to attend her paternal grandmother's funeral, someone she had not bonded with due to distance and a separation from Jackson because they didn't get along. So, I wanted them to meet my mother. I figured what this dysfunctional English/Irish southern family needed to bring them all closer to their emotions was an Italian grandmother. Did it go well? She and Jackson fell in love with one another when they met. She actually had me bring in her bags from my car so she could stay at Jackson's house for the holiday. My mother, but she wanted to stay at Jackson's house. I was very happy that they got along so well and yes; I was willing to take a back seat to their relationship, because they were happy. Her approval was everything to me. Now I felt I could relax and take this relationship serious, because it had a future on firm ground. What did I tell you? The only son of an Italian mother. She has a powerful role in her son's life until the day that he dies, not her.

By the end of Easter dinner, the three of them were as thick as thieves. Out came Jackson's photo albums, his daughter sat on my mother's lap while mom brushed her hair, and on and on. She told them stories about my childhood. It went on for days. I went back to work and my mother still hadn't even seen my apartment. She was very content to stay right where she was, at Jackson's house, thank you. So, since he lived so close to where I worked (I could walk to the office from his house), I would go over every day at lunch and talk with her, and we'd all get together for dinner and I'd stay and chat with her and watch TV, or Jackson and I would go somewhere for dinner and if she didn't want to come, she'd stay at the house with his daughter and they'd "chat." I was so happy that his daughter had an older woman in her life that she could bond with and love. That girl was an aching heart in motion, always. I loved the sight of her, though. As far as I was concerned, she was MY daughter. Her parents were both so busy advancing their careers they never seemed to notice this little kid, all eyes and legs, wanting to be noticed and loved. I scooped her right up and she became my buddy, my best friend. I don't think a day went by that I didn't see her at her father's or talk with her on the phone; we had clicked that easily. Believe me; it did not start out that way. After she met me, one day her father was taking her home and he asked her to rate me on a scale from 1 to 10, 10 being the highest. Without missing a beat, she said, "Zero." I had to laugh when he told me because I surmised from that, that she knew how serious her father was in his feelings for me and that I was going to become a part of his everyday life. At that point, I also realized that we had to become friends, not enemies. I wanted her to know that she would not be losing her father again, because I came into the picture. I wanted her to know that she was going to be a part of this picture too, and now had two men who loved and adored her. I would always be there for her the next 10+ years, and even today, I still think of her and refer to her in conversation as my stepdaughter. A great kid. But, back to Easter.

My mother and I had this zany idea. We decided that we would go out the night before Easter and buy Easter baskets for Jackson and his daughter, something we would make ourselves, and surprise them Easter morning. Off we go to Wegman's, the local supplier of everything that life requires. God, what we didn't buy that night. Basically, everything that was left in stock, cleaned the shelves, we did. We had a blast. We took it all home and started creating their Easter baskets, like my parents did when we were kids. I enjoyed it because I never could figure out growing up how my parents could put together so much stuff for the four of us children. Now I knew. And believe me, I've used that creativity ever since, on many different occasions. So, we waited until Jackson was in bed and I dragged everything into the basement. He left us alone because he thought that we were going to sit up and talk for the night, catching up on family things. Instead, once he was "out," we snuck down into the basement and tore everything apart and started the process of creating their Easter baskets. It actually took only about an hour for each basket, but by the time we were through yakking and laughing, it was almost 4:00 a.m. But, my mother and I had a ball in that basement. Talking about my growing up and the memories that doing this brought back for her. See, my sisters never did this sort of thing with my mother, so she was never able to share this part of her history with them. Whereas, when we got together, my mother and I would make sauce and meatballs, or homemade macaroni, or bake bread, make lasagna, and all the while we'd be talking. I learned more about my mother's life by being in the kitchen with her, helping her prep and cook. If you think MY life is interesting, you should have met my mother. Now, there's a book. Oh, my God, I remember once making bread with her and discovering that she'd had a miscarriage between having my older sister and me. My sisters never knew this. That's what happens when you stick around and bond with your parents. I also learned how to cook in the process. And she loved nothing more than to hear me sing. So, we'd prep everything for the sauce or stuffed peppers and all the while she would be saying, "Now, sing 'My Buddy.' That was your grandmother's favorite song." So, I'd stand there and sing while we cooked. It seemed very natural to me, and I always sing now when I cook. I feel closer to her, now that she's gone. Anyway, we finally finished the baskets (They were BIG suckers, too) and we hid them. When Jackson went to pick up his daughter on Easter morning, we hauled out the baskets and set them both on the dining room table with Easter cards for them. When they came in, "Oh, my God." His daughter was breathless. No one had ever done something like that for her before. I cannot tell you how grateful this little girl was for anything that someone would do for her. And, I have never known anyone who loved to laugh more than that girl. She was, and is, incredible. A shining light in my life, always. So, everyone had a happy Easter. Jackson loved to cook; so he got the chance to cook with my mother. It was interesting. Southern fried meets Italian baked. He was very kind and patient with her and she taught him whatever he wanted to know, which was usually my favorite dishes, because she had gone to cooking school during WW2, and they clicked. I am telling you that I saw love bloom that Easter day between the two of them. I swear, Jackson found the mother he had always been looking for; someone who would kid and joke with him, or tell him how good his cooking was, or pat him on the back while he was doing something she had taught him in the kitchen and take his face in her hands and kiss him on the cheek. In that sense, Jackson was like his daughter. They both craved being loved and accepted and that required an Italian mother. I am sorry, but there is something to be said about an Italian mother, when she wraps her arms around you and tells you how wonderful you are. At that moment, you know that you are her entire life. It is the most wonderful feeling. Well, Jackson and his daughter got to experience that. Apparently, his mother was this pencil-thin, very stoic and withdrawn person, and the maternal grandmother was always very critical of her. Not a good mix. Then, they met mom. My mother was sort of an Italian Mary Poppins, I guess. Very sweet and loving, a great sense of humor, sort of heavyset but always had a figure and the greatest legs I've ever seen on a woman. God how she loved to dance. I must tell you about my mother, because it bears telling, and will later on in the story.

One interesting aspect about Jackson was his lack of faith and how he was sort of mesmerized by my Catholicism. It seemed very natural to me, having been raised in "the faith." You just did it. You went to Mass and you prayed at home, using your rosary. He used to tell me, "God, how you work those beads." I did what my mother had done and taught all of her children to do. She was a great believer in the rosary as a source of patience and an instrument whose use enabled you to focus during times of stress. I still use them. I must tell you a story here about the power of faith. After my mother had been diagnosed with Alzheimer's, she came to stay with us. One day, I walked into the living room and there she was, sitting on the couch, rubbing her fingers together in this rhythmic motion. I asked her if anything was wrong and she told me no, that she was saying her rosary. I said, "Mom, there's nothing in your hands." Of course she looked at me as if I were nuts. And, she told me that she knew that. Her rosary beads had broken, so she was doing them from memory. I couldn't believe it. There she sat, moving invisible beads through her fingers, citing the decades of the Lord's Prayer and the Hail Mary, through the memory of how it felt holding her rosary beads in her hands. To me, she was an incredible woman. Another brief story. I never received Confirmation until after my mother passed away. This was a great source of pain for her, but I never did get confirmed. Rebellion on my part. The year after she died, I attended classes at my church and finally, at 41, I received my Confirmation. I remember standing at the altar in church afterward while being received into the community, and asking my mother if I had finally made her happy, if she could finally rest in peace. That night, my mother came to me in a dream. She took me by the hand into a room and there were all of my relatives, dear aunts and uncles and my wonderful grandfather who had all passed away, and she showed me that they were celebrating my Confirmation. She had a huge smile and said to me, "Look," and pointed at everyone with her hand and how they had all gathered and were toasting me and celebrating. When I woke up, I felt such exhilaration, and it lasted for days. It was as if I had actually been in her presence. I couldn't get over the feeling of her touching my arm and walking me into the room where everyone had gathered. When I told my priest about it, he said that I had been in the presence of spirit that she had actually come to me to let me know how happy I had made her. I will never forget that dream as long as I live. My mother has come to me many times in my dreams with different messages, but that one was so filled with happiness and love that I will always remember it, specifically.

I held out for about six months, as I remember it going. I'm talking about sex. I take sex as a very serious issue in a relationship. By now, Dell and I had been apart for almost a year, and I was still physically "attached" to him. What to do? Call mom. My mother was always a great one for advice. So, she told me, "Son, you have to let go. Sit down some time and pretend that you're talking with Dell, and say good-bye to him." Sounded noodles to me, but I tucked it away. However, she had planted a seed. I started to think that I wasn't being fair to Jackson because I still cared and grieved over Dell. Jackson and I had a long talk and I opened up to him emotionally and told him that I would try my best and we'd see what happened. He said that he understood and would wait. He waited about six months. At that point, he was starting to walk funny, so I started browbeating myself into doing this - "do it. You know you love him and you know that he loves you. It's been six freakin' months since you talked with him about it. What the hell are you waiting for??" We had been tested and both results were negative, so I couldn't use that one anymore. It was that instinct that I talked about in the beginning of the story. There was something within me that was holding back, telling me to hold back, but I began telling myself that I didn't want to let go of Dell and that wasn't fair to Jackson. Again, "Poor Jackson". So, we did it. One night we went to bed and I excused myself, went downstairs to the living room and sat there "talking with Dell," as my mother had said to do, and I said goodbye to him, and I cried. I went upstairs and got back into bed and Jackson asked me if I "talked with Dell," and I said that I had and Jackson basically attacked me. I really didn't know what the hell hit me. One minute, we were lying there, talking and the next whoosh. You see, Jackson had a waterbed and when he lunged at me, he made this incredible wave, and out I went. When I climbed back in, I was laughing so hard I couldn't talk. I soon realized that he wasn't in the mood for talking. He was waiting. And Pounced. He's a Leo. Never mind about his voice. In bed, that man had an entire arsenal with him. I didn't stand a chance. It was like the Marines landing at Iwo Jima. You make any man wait six months for sex and see what happens, IF he's still hangin' around, ok? Get back to me on that one. There's a survey in itself. That one task. Go for it. I dare ya. That night alone I could title separately and market - "Stories My Mother Never Told Me." Anyway, I gather you get the idea that we hit if off in the sack. Never any problem there, I assure you. Once we started, we were at it like rabbits. Two, three, four times a day. We made up for lost time and then some. I had no complaints. Those southern boys are, as a friend of mine says, "Some kinda shit." It must be the humidity, I swear. Oh, that's right, you didn't know. Jackson was not my first southern boy. No, no. I had me a boy from 'bama before Jackson. Now, you wanna talk "Deep South," and what THAT means, let's do lunch. I'll even pay. That boy could have taught Jackson a couple a' things. Not much, though. But, there was one guy I dated that had it all over them. He was 6' 4", a dancer in LA when I was there studying acting. His name was Tom and he was, well still is, black. I will say one thing. It was the only time I passed out in bed. Amen. Oh, yes. The eggs in MY basket have many colors. Variete, as the French say. Ten years after Tom and I broke up, I went to LA to visit a friend. While I was there, I prayed to St. Jude to let me see Tom, to make sure he was all right after all the years that had passed. One day, while sitting at a light on Hollywood Boulevard, a man passed right in front of my car while crossing the street. It was

Tom! I turned the corner and parked about half a block down from where he was walking, got out of my car and waited for him to pass by, staring at him, knowing he had no idea who I was. Well, come on! Ten years had passed! Actually, I looked better! As he approached me, I said, "Hello, Tom. I can't believe it's you!" He stopped and looked at me as if he knew me from somewhere, but wasn't quite sure. Then I laughed. He knew exactly who I was and started jumping up and down and yelling on the boulevard. What a damn miracle that was! We spent the next two days together, totally alone. It was nonstop catching up. And, he still had only one thing on his mind when he saw me. That Devil. Begged me to forget going back to France, to stay in LA and move in with him. And I'll bet you're thinking that this sort of thing only happens to women. Wrong. Men get shafted, too. As Alberta Hunter used to say, "Later." I'm telling you ladies, gay or straight, men are dogs. Just that simple. I should have listened to that little voice in the back of my head and here's why...

Chapter Three

"What IS This Thing Called Love?"

O ne day, while I was cleaning Jackson's house, I was putting his clean laundry in the bedroom closet. As I pulled open the sock drawer in his closet, something fell to the floor from underneath the drawer. I picked it up. It was a card. Somebody named "Joe" was thanking my "J" for a great time. Unfortunately, the great time had by "Joe" was the week prior to my finding the card. Read on, MacDuff. So, I did. This "Joe" was describing how it feels when my "J's" hands are on him. Well, this was going to require a chair, a cigarette, and a thorough cleaning of that friggin' sock drawer. I put Oprah on "record" and went back to the infamous sock drawer. Oh, those moments in life when time literally stands still and the only active thing you recall is the sound of your own heartbeat pounding in your ears. He was having an affair?? No, I must be wrong. My Jackson??? There's some mistake. This must be an old card. It took me about two milliseconds to rip the damn drawer out of the closet, along with the other three drawers. As I thought, cards hidden everywhere, 15 in all that I found. Luckily, they were all from the same person. This somebody named "Joe." Now, why did that ring a familiar bell?? "Joe." There was only one envelope that he'd saved. Why? Ask him. I have no idea. Now the bell went off. "Joe" was a guy named J.F. I had met him at a party. He and my Jackson had gone off to the other side of the room and were talking, about what Jackson never told me. Guess I know now, don't I? I suddenly felt very sick to my stomach. So much for cleaning the house that day. I left all of the cards on his bed, went downstairs to the den and waited, staring out the window, waiting for his car to pull into the driveway. Here we were in the thick of the AIDS epidemic, and he's having a friggin' affair. Sweet Mother in Heaven. When he came in, he didn't see me, and he headed upstairs to his bedroom. "Hon? Where are you?" I heard him walk into his bedroom. Total silence. "Shit. J. Where are you?" He ran back downstairs and saw me sitting in the den. And the tears, they flowed like wine. Not mine. Jackson's. I have never known anyone to turn on the taps as quick as that guy. He would gush with one look from me. It was embarrassing because I never took his crying serious; it came so easy to him. Then he saw my suitcase. The monsoon really kicked into overdrive. Yes, I had packed what belongings were mine at Jackson's house, and I sat there and waited for him. "Okay, I'm listening. You had better stop crying and start explaining."

Jackson went on to tell me that J.F. was someone that he had been seeing before he'd met me and he had broken it off when we started dating regularly, but J.F. kept calling him at work and wanting to meet him for lunch and apparently when they did, it always somehow turned into a sexual liaison, and since Jackson and I were not having sex at the time. See, I told you, all men are dogs. "So, what you're telling me is that last week's 'lunch' was another round of having sex in his office with the door locked of course, so his secretary wouldn't interrupt. Do I have that right, Jackson?" "She was at lunch." "Is that the only part that I got wrong, Jackson?" "Yes." "Thank you. So, the fact that we are surrounded by people dying from AIDS and the fact that I waited to have sex with you because I felt that I was being unfair to you because of my past relationship with Dell, you're telling me that you used that as your reasoning for having sex with someone else, even though you told me that you understood what I was going through and would wait. Thank you, again." And, I got up and walked out the door, suitcase in hand. He stood there crying, begging me to stay, to try and understand. The only thing that I was trying to understand at that moment was how I got into such a mess and why hadn't I listened to that little voice telling me to wait. I threw my suitcase into the back seat and got into my car and went home. My home. I paced and I yelled and I told myself what an idiot I was, but that it was early, and there wasn't that much of me invested yet. Or, so I thought. Poor Missie, my little poodle. She walked right alongside me in the apartment, keeping up with my pace, letting out a little moan, telling me she understood and she was still with me. As if to say, "We have the world by the balls, boss. We're gonna be fine, but no more fuckups, okay?" I was angrier with myself than at Jackson, for putting him before my own better judgment. So, I went back to my life; working in the office and having lunch with friends or co-workers, going to Frank's and Pat's house for Sunday breakfast as was our usual arrangement, and maybe a trip out to Clarence to the flea market early Sunday mornings. Anything to get back to my normal routine. I wanted nothing to do with Jackson. I had decided to listen to that voice in my head. I also decided to have another AIDS test, too.

The phone started ringing. It got to the point where I picked it up and set it back on the receiver, or took it off of the hook and would go downstairs to my landlord's if I needed to make a call. One night at about 2:00 a.m., my doorbell started ringing. I'm thinking, "I'll kill him." I lay there, waiting for it to stop. Missie starts yapping at the window. I hear Jackson out in the yard, yelling up to my bedroom window, in the rain. "Please, open the door." Of course, he was crocked. I hate dealing with drunks. My father was an alcoholic and I see red when I'm dealing with someone who's drunk. Drives me right up the wall. So, I got up and went to the window. "Go home, you idiot. Go back to J.F. and wake him up!" I had to grab Missie and put her on the bed to shut her trap. SLAM goes my window. "Please let me in." No. "Please!!!!" Go to hell!!! Then the crying started.

Oh, my God. The crying and wailing out in the yard and it's already going for 2:30 a.m. My landlord starts knocking on the ceiling. The phone rings. It's my landlord, Gary... "Hi. This is very romantic and all that bullshit but I have to work in the morning. Let the guy in, okay?" Down I go stomping all the way, ready for blood, I pull open the damn door and there he is, sitting on the steps, crying and crying, soaking wet from the rain. Poor Jackson (See what I mean?). "Come on. Get up. You idiot, you woke up Gary. Happy now? Get in here." Now when Jackson cries, you have to understand that he cries like a little kid. He tries talking and he's all stutters and sputters and sighs and trembling lips and the tears are pouring like the friggin' monsoon. I walked him up the steps and held his hand so he wouldn't trip. Of course Missie, the little traitor that she is, is right behind us all the way jumping and barking running in circles at the top of the steps because look, "Daddy's here." Yea? Shut up, traitor!!! Under the couch she goes with her head sticking out not missing a trick. I get him situated in the living room, grab a towel and dry his hair and hang up his coat to dry, and I put on the coffee (So much for sleeping). Jackson: "You can't do this. We had such a great start. Why are you ending it now?" (Why am I ending it?). How it is that men can do that switch and all of a sudden it's what you are doing that's the problem?? Where do they get that?? Their mothers??? "Now dear, you remember what mother taught you. When you're a big strong man, you dump all the blame onto your partner. Always make it their fault and you'll be happy as a pig in shit, Pumpkin. Make Mother proud now." What crap!!!! "Jackson, this isn't going to work. I can't trust you. Why don't you get that part of it? It isn't what I'm doing that's the problem. You're the one having the affair, remember?" "But, I tried, I really tried not to do it. I tried to stay away from him." "Jackson, what are you saying? Am I supposed to suddenly understand here? Okay, I understand what you're saying. You're weak. You can't stay away from him. Fine. Then, stay away from me. That's the answer, Jackson. You cannot have both." So, as he sat there with his head in his hands wrapped in a towel, sniffling, I got up and went and got him a cup of coffee. "Jackson, you know you can't drink. You get plowed on 1 beer, for Christ's sake. Come on, come into the kitchen and have some coffee." No answer. "Jackson?" Ain't nothin' happenin'. I ran into the living room and the S.O.B. was passed out on the couch. No!!!! Nothing but snoring. "Jackson!! Jackson!!!!!!!" And there's Missie, sniffing under the towel, licking his face, and still nothing. Well, nothing to do but to cover him and get into bed and try to get some sleep for work in the morning. Didn't the snake slither in about an hour later and climb into bed, naked, with me. "It's cold on the couch". I jumped up and I'm hitting him without even knowing what the hell I'm doing. "What are you doing to me, Jackson?? Why did you have to go and ruin everything with that slut?? You son-of-a-bitch! How could you do this?" He didn't yell, he didn't hit back, he put his arms around me and held me and let me hit him and let me cry and kept saying over and over, "I'm so sorry J. I'm so sorry. I do love you. I'm very confused by this. I didn't expect to fall in love with someone so soon. I'm so sorry. Please forgive me, please. I don't want to go back home without you. Please say you forgive me. I can't take this anymore. Please." Over and over how sorry he was.

Of course, the strange thing about that night was that it created a pattern in our relationship that continued until the very end. Our most passionate lovemaking always took place after an incident like this. The truth? We fit in every aspect. We really did. There wasn't an area I can recall in which we initially had a problem. I loved Jackson in the beginning because he had qualities that I admired in a man. No matter how difficult the situation or what price he would end up paying, he always told me the truth. He was quiet and loving and gentle with me. He realized that I had had a difficult time with Dell and with leaving Dell because of his illness. He understood all of that and never put any sort of pressure on me. He respected my feelings about all of it. He enjoyed being with me because I always made him laugh and I made him my center of attention. Or, we would have very difficult conversations for him about his family, which he appreciated because he wanted to express these feelings but didn't quite know how. That impressed me as well, because Jackson wasn't a person to open up easily with people, especially about very personal issues, and that he would do it with me showed me that he trusted me and wanted to become closer to me. In the beginning, we had fun and enjoyed being together and being with his daughter. Not lots of money to spend on crazy weekends in the country or dining out a lot. No, being home and cooking together, talking about our day, maybe having friends over, but usually just the two of us and his daughter, when she would do her sleepover, and it was the three of us. It was a wonderful beginning, and I realized that I actually had invested more of myself than I realized and I didn't want to throw that away. I didn't want to have her feel that she was being thrown away, either. I agreed to come back, if he promised never to see J.F. again. He promised. I went back to Jackson's house two days later. Then began the tender moments, probably the nicest time of our relationship. You know, the time spent together of falling in love and knowing it and welcoming it.

Autumn was here and we would spend hours in the living room with the fireplace ablaze and we would stretch out on the floor together and talk or listen to music and always make love. Some beautifully tender moments that I'll never forget. Or, we would go for long walks in the park or drive out to the lake and listen to the waves. We would talk about our future together and what we wanted to do, where we wanted to go. We were committing ourselves to one another and nothing was an obstacle. We were going to do this together; face the world and watch each other's backs.

I had a secret that I had told Jackson about when we realized that we were growing closer to one another early on in our relationship. I had been raped when I was about ten years old and had been exposed to the hepatitis B virus. I was what was called a chronic carrier, which meant that it wasn't a threat to my health but I could expose other people through my blood or semen. So, I was always very aware of any intimacy that may come up and when it was heading that way with Jackson, I made sure to sit him down and tell him. It was no problem for him. He told me, "It comes with you. I love you. I'll get the inoculations. No more problem." I loved him even more for that because I dread having to tell anyone about it because it reminds me of a part of my past I wanted to forget. There is a certain shame that comes with carrying a contagious disease, no matter how you came by its exposure to you. It just does. I know that I will love that man forever for accepting me as I was and never, ever making an issue of my health in all the years that we were together, until the end. For that, I thank you, Jackson.

It was a Saturday afternoon and Jackson decided that we should take a drive. Okay. There was an antique's shop he'd heard about and he wanted to investigate. Fine with me. I love antiques. So, in we go and we're looking around. A really nice older couple owned the shop and we chatted with them about the business and how long they'd been in it. Really nice, down-to-earth people. Well, I was browsing; not buying and eventually I told Jackson that I was going to head out to the car and have a cigarette. He could take his time. About 20 minutes later, he came out and he handed me a bag. For me? Yep, for you. In it was a little box and in the box was this beautiful amethyst man's ring with a silver engraved band. Very Victorian. What I loved about it was the amethyst had a raised cameo engraved on the top of the stone. It was absolutely beautiful. "I want you to wear this as a sign of our commitment to one another. Will you do that?" Oh, yea. Oh, it was beautiful. For 11 years, I never took off that ring. Never. Not in the hospital, not in the emergency rooms, not doing the dishes, not while cleaning the house, not while doing the gardening or shoveling the snow. Not until after he left. And, only then to send it back to him. That was the hardest thing for me to do. It let me know that it was over. I couldn't keep it. Jackson thought that I was being petty and spiteful, but that's not true. I couldn't keep the ring, not after the way things ended. But, that's much later in the story, when things went terribly wrong for us. For now, we were happy. I used to love waking up in the morning and finding him there, staring at me. What a strange feeling. He used to say that I had no idea how attractive I was, especially when I was sleeping, and he would wake up early on the weekends and lay there, looking at me sleep. Now, how can you NOT love a guy who loves you even when you're sleeping?? My favorite thing was to watch Jackson attack a project of some sort. His level of intensity was incredible to watch. His face would scrunch all up and the tip of his tongue would pop out through his lips, furrowed eyebrows and all, one cellular mass of focus and ability. I don't think I have ever focused on one particular thing at a time in my entire life, except maybe for Jackson. But that was pure pleasure for me. I was proud of him and I wanted him to succeed and was willing to do whatever I had to in order for him to achieve his dreams. His dreams became mine.

As time went on, Jackson decided to get out from under debt by selling his house. He and his ex-wife had come to terms with their divorce settlement and he wanted to clear himself of some debt hanging over his head from his marriage and I think begin again. We set about fixing up his house. It was one of those saltboxes that were built by the millions across America after World War II, by returning GI's for their new families. We began painting and repairing, doing what we could ourselves. I took on the task of tearing out a built-in hutch that ran the length of a wall in his dining room, so he would have more space in the room, itself. We went at it like gangbusters and when his daughter came over she grabbed a sledgehammer and clobbered that built-in for all it was worth. We had a ball that day. In about a month's time, we basically had the place done. The worst part was the bathroom. He insisted I paint it this Pepto-Bismol® pink. His tastes could be extreme, but it was his bathroom. I still can't chug Pepto-Bismol®, though. We stayed for a few months in my apartment after the sale of his house, and took our time looking for a place. We came upon a very nice apartment in an old Victorian house. We had the second floor. As it was, another pattern began in our relationship at this time. Jackson had been promoted to a management position and went to England on business for his company and I took charge of the move. My friend Gary, my former landlord, helped me move our belongings into the apartment and I lived there for about a month before Jackson returned home.

At that point, we went searching for furniture. Listen, you really get to know someone when you watch him spend money. I stepped back and observed, because it was Jackson's money going into the new furniture, so I figured it should be him doing the choosing. Oh, my God. Everything was either whorehouse red or Chinese lacquer, or glass top with chrome bases. Cringe? I couldn't believe it. He seemed so quiet. Where did this come from?? I somehow managed to turn his attention toward some pickled ash for the bedroom (Of course, to satisfy him, it had to come with mirrors for above the bed). The set had a four-poster bed and huge armoire with double dresser. A beautiful collection. He won out on the dining room, which was a beveled glass top number with pink and gold chrome swirls for legs and pink (Again that damn pink) upholstered chairs with skirts. Don't worry. His cat soon took care of the skirts on the chairs with his claws. Thank you, Shadow. I blended the antique pieces I was collecting with what he had bought; an Empire card table in the living room and an early American lady's writing desk in the hall under a modern mirror, an oil painting here or there, an old-fashioned coffee grinder in the kitchen along with my McCoy cookie jars. A couple of flow-blue plates here and there, a Victorian fainting couch in the guest bedroom. That sort of thing, pieces here and there, to break up the austerity of all brand new furniture. Something to give it a sense of time and the anchoring that aged wood gives to a room. All in all, not bad for a starter couple.

When everything was said and done, and in place, we decided to have a housewarming party. Oh my God, I think we ended up with invites to 75-80 people, and they were all allowed to bring a guest. Thank God I remembered to stagger the invites.

I think it ran 25 at half-hour intervals. Everyone showed up and everyone seemed to bring at least one person with them. Jackson and I had cooked for days - all recipes on which we had grown up, so there was a ton of southern fried chicken, sweet potato soufflé, peach pie and apple cobbler from Jackson; lasagna, antipasto, meatballs, huge salads, fresh-baked bread and so on from me. Tons of liquor and wine, and everyone had a ball. We timed it for a Friday night, between 7-10, so that everyone could head out to the bars and finish their carousing there. That's a great idea if you're planning a party. And, I made sure that his daughter was there, to be introduced and meet everyone. She was the prima ballerina that night. As I remember, she and I ended up changing and cleaning up the aftermath while her father collapsed in the living room. But, we were finally "introduced" into the community as a family. The bonding had taken place. She knew that I wasn't out to take her away from her father and that I loved her as she was and thought of her as mine.

The late 80's/early 90's were a great time to live in Rochester. It was just on the cusp of the disaster that was to befall that charming city, involving several huge employers in the region. That nightmare had yet to become a reality. In other words, it was still a fun place to live. Lots of energy and lots to offer young people and children. Wonderful parks, the lakefront, museums, art galleries, the science museum, free summer concerts, beautiful architecture, the wine country, etc. And, a large, wealthy, and active gay community. A great place to live. Plus, there was Jackson's house. This little saltbox of a thing built after World War II for some soldier and his bride. At one point, the garage had been enclosed and turned into a study/TV room. Three bedrooms and a bath upstairs. His daughter's bedroom was an add-on, over what had been the garage, and it was sort of incomplete. You know, it was always a mess and had her toys and dolls, etc., but it didn't seem permanent. So, I set about making it her room. I re-arranged the furniture and bought window treatments more in line for a girl her age, but it needed something to anchor it and make it hers. I had this old steamer trunk that I plopped in there for her "private" things: her journals, and pictures, etc. I always felt that she had no privacy and I wanted her to have some. I had a collection of stuffed animals that I'd had for years, mainly Teddy bears that I'd collected from all over, and I popped the lid of the trunk and stuffed them into the upper tray so that they were flopping out all over the top of the trunk. It made her feel as if whenever she walked into the room, there they all were, waiting for her to return. She loved it. Shortly after Jackson and I met, his roommate moved out and in with my friend Lee (Actually, they are still together). So, that bedroom sat empty. I finally threw some spare antiques I had in there; a cannonball rope bed, a settee, a free-standing mirror, and a Queen Anne library chair, to give it a sense of being used. I never touched Jackson's bedroom, only to clean it. That room was a total disaster, waterbed and all, but I felt that it was his space to do with as he chose. We were becoming a unit, the three of us, and I finally felt that I was part of a family, a family that wanted me. It was a nice feeling.

Chapter Four

**"Some Things You Will Mourn Until The Day
You Die. It's Just A Given..."
JMB**

J ackson began traveling a lot for his company, always to
Europe, mainly England and then France. On one return trip
from France, he came home and was very quiet. Quick to pick up
on this sort of thing, I asked him if he wanted to talk with me and
he told me that he did. An opportunity had come up for him to
take a one-year assignment with his company in France. Rouen,
to be exact. Never heard of it. "It's north of Paris. I would have to
leave in a month's time and stay for the year." Let me pick up my
heart before it gets mud tracked on it, okay? "Is this something
that you really want to do? Will it help with your career to go
there for a year?" "Yes, it will. It will give me leverage in dealing
with the home office, which is in England, if I have some
international experience under my belt and I have to do it now
before I get any older. If I'm going to achieve the goal of a vice-
presidency in ten years, it starts now." I held his hand and bit my
tongue while he talked because of course in my brain I was
screaming, "No!!! Don't do it!!!!" That voice in the back of my
head was going full throttle. Instead, I held his hand and realized
that he was right and that this was what we had planned on doing

and we had to get started. He was already in his mid-thirties. No spring chicken in the world of corporate America. There were younger guys coming in already snapping at his heels where he worked. I could tell by his voice that this was going to be a solo act. "You're going to go alone, aren't you?" He looked at me and shook his head, saying, "I'm going to have to. I have to get my bearings there first and get settled into the routine. But you can come and visit and stay for three months at a time. That's what the law allows." "What about the lease on the apartment? I can't afford this on my salary. Will they let us out of the lease?" "You're going to stay here. This is our home. I've figured things out financially (Already, Jackson?) and I'll pay the rent on the apartment and you can use your paycheck for the other bills; you know, the utilities, your food, the car." "Jackson, you're sure this is how you want to do this? I would understand if you wanted to separate now." "No. Is that what you want?" I told him, "Never. I want you to know that you can do this solo, if you want." "No. I want what I have and I want to be able to come back to all of this and have you here. Will that be too hard for you to do?" "Jackson, the day will never come when I will leave you. I love you." We proceeded to prepare for his leaving. Things had to be set up. Bank accounts had to have access with both our names, so I could pay things for him while he was living in France. Both our names were on the lease, so that wasn't a problem. I had to be put into his will, in case something happened to him in Europe. He wanted to make sure that if something should happen, his family couldn't come in and throw me out. It's happened to others. I've known men to end up out on the street when their lovers have died and families have stepped in. The law then didn't recognize lovers and they haven't come that far in all these years. So, Jackson made sure that I was protected in his will. Mind you, this was in the early 90s, so there wasn't a lot of terrorism in this country to worry about. Not the nightmare it is now to travel. I went and applied for a passport. We bought Jackson luggage and items that he would need for living in France that would be cheaper to buy here, until he got settled;

everyday things which can be very expensive in Europe; soap, detergent, towels, underwear, an alarm clock, toothpaste, socks, sneakers. We got him all stocked up and when it came time loaded up the entire luggage. And yes, I began to dread the passing of the days. It went by so quickly. One week, two weeks. My mother came up for a visit and to say goodbye to Jackson. Oh, how she cried. You would have thought he was going off to a war. She never left his side. She'd wait at the window in the afternoons, looking down the street, waiting to see Jackson's car coming. Nothing swayed her from her post. I love Italian mothers. Once you're in their heart, you're there for life. His daughter came and spent a week with us to be with her dad and my mom. That lost little girl. People always coming and going in her life. Jackson would take her to the lake and they would walk along the lakefront, talking, or we would take her out shopping and to restaurants and my mom would brush her hair and help her with her homework at night and I'd run her to school in the morning. I wanted her to know that I would still be there for her, whenever she needed me. Three weeks had gone by. Mom left. His daughter went home. Where did it go? SLOW DOWN! Then came the morning to drive him to the airport. It was like the day they brought JFK back from Dallas. I dreaded every minute of it. Well, not every minute. When we woke up, we made love. We had breakfast and, we made love again. We showered and made love in the shower. We dressed and somehow ended up...making love. All this before noon. You know, there's an intensity to making love when you know it may be your last. I remember thinking that I needed to remember how smooth his skin was when I ran my hand across his back and how he breathed and in the silence, the sound of his heart beating. But, we were running out of time. He had to take a flight to NYC and catch his flight to Paris. He had shipped some of the luggage ahead, the company paying for whatever he wanted to take to Rouen. They had a flat that he could use while he looked for his own apartment, and would pay for storage of his things until he was settled. Corporate America is a world unto itself. You may think that they're bleeding you dry while you're working for them, but the "bennies" are incredible. So, I sat on the bed with Missie and watched him dress for his flight, while he stared back at me in the mirror. I kept thinking, "God, I want to remember this." It was time to leave for the airport. I remember feeling so torn that day. I was heartbroken. "Time to go." He had become my best friend, as well as my lover. I shared everything with Jackson. I sought his counsel on so many things. In a way, his having the affair was a good thing, because it taught us how precious what we had really was and our love for one another seemed stronger. It had been tested and challenged and had survived. I can say that I was actually happier after the affair because what we had worked. Of course all of our friends thought that we were nuts. "A year?? This is going to die a quick death. Be prepared. Dump him now, less heartache." They were worried for us, I know. I thank God every day that I have the strong network of friends that I have been given. A safety net? You can bet your ass on that one, Sherlock. Anyway, we had to say goodbye at the apartment. Not a chance we'd be locking lips at the airport. I think I almost choked him to death; I had such a tight hold on him. Poor Jackson. He didn't want to get upset and be bleary-eyed and sniffling at the airport, but I couldn't help it, I couldn't let go of him that day. I never felt myself to be a complete person again until he came home from Europe for good and that would take four long years; not one, but four. We got to the airport and I waited with him, talking crap to fill the void, but I couldn't take my eyes from him. We sat next to one another and looked at the floor and at each other. At one point, Jackson wrote, "I love you," in the palm of my hand. I know, but when it's happening to you, it's always different and special and sweet, okay? They called the flight and it was really time to say goodbye to one another. I actually started getting anxious, looking around and holding onto his coat sleeve so he couldn't get in line to board, and asking him to stay, not to do this, stay here and we'll figure something else out, but don't do this, don't go, not now, maybe tomorrow okay?; or maybe next week, but not now, *please* Jackson. He finally turned around and gave me this incredibly tight hug and I've never forgotten what he whispered, "This is for us. You take care of you for me while I'm gone, okay? Remember, I love you and I'm coming back and we'll never be apart again. I promise." And, he was gone. You know how it feels when something is ripped from your arms? That sudden void you feel? That ache that never leaves. Again, how the hell did I ever get home? Don't remember a thing until I hit our bed and cried and cried and cried. Just me and Missie now. She jumped up on the bed and licked my face and whimpered, not knowing what to do to help. Sometimes, I think that I miss that dear sweet dog more than I miss Jackson. Yes, Missie is gone.

I have been fortunate in that the type of work I do has crossed over from being that of an office job to being an at-home profession. It's heaven to roll out of bed in the a.m., no shower, no shave, no traffic, no bosses, no attitudes to deal with, no weather to protect yourself from; just move your butt from one room to the next and start typing. And, that's what I did. I kept busy with work. I also sold my car. No point, as Jackson said, in having two cars now. A friend of mine from my days of working in a hospital in town was moving to Texas and bought my car. Time to start conserving. For the first year, I wrote Jackson at least once a week. My letters were journals of my time spent that week and I'd always mail them on Friday, because he would always call me on Saturday afternoon, after he did his laundry. Like clockwork, that boy. What a creature of habit. And, he never missed a phone call in four years. Not to say that I didn't use Ma Bell as well. Whoa. At one point, I paid Sprint $1000 for one month. Were they happy. But, I worked for it and I spent it as I wanted, and that was to hear Jackson's voice. I've never thought that it was money wasted, then or now. You have to do what you have to do. After a while, we developed this weird psychic connection. For about a week one time, I kept waking up at 7 a.m. right on the dot, never an alarm going off, have my eyes pop open for no reason that I could discover. So, the following weekend I mentioned to Jackson how strange it was but every morning that week I woke right up at 7 a.m. Well, he roared. "How is this funny?" "I have been doing an exercise at work. Every morning I set the clock on my desk at work to go off when it's at 6:58 a.m. your time. I sit at my desk and focus my mind on you. Guess it really works, huh?" I would also have dreams about Jackson and would call, or have him call me to tell me he had been robbed walking down the street, or had been in a fender bender the night before. Oh, I can't forget to tell you this story. When Jackson first went to France, as I said, he used to call every Saturday afternoon. I had gone to Pennsylvania one week because my mother was ill and when I came back, I shut off the ringer and lowered the volume on the answering machine so I could sleep that night, having to work the following morning. Well, I forgot to turn up the volume the next morning and turn on the ringer. One day, two days, three days. Finally, my friend Bruce stopped by and wanted to know where I'd been because he had left several messages and hadn't heard from me.

THE PHONE!!!!!................... As soon as he mentioned it, I corrected the problem. When I looked at the answering machine, I had almost 20 phone calls. So, I hit the "rewind" and I'm listening. The usual; my friend Frank telling me that he was going to Toronto for a few days and would call when he got back, my friend Eva letting me know that she'd made it safely to Texas, Bruce's phone calls. There's a call from Jackson, "Hi, hon. I thought I'd call because I miss you. I'll talk with you tomorrow, okay? Love ya. Bye." Click...another call from Jackson, the following day..."Hi, hon. What's up? Where've you been? Now, I'll call you tomorrow. Love ya. Bye." Click...another call from Jackson, the following day..."J, where ARE you? I'm going to call you back in the morning. I love you. Bye." Click...(Oh, Dear)...another call from Jackson, the following morning..."J........... WHERE ARE YOU???............ Now, he's crying and trying to talk and he's choking up and stuttering. WHAT'S HAPPENED?? I CAN'T FIND YOU.... WHAT'S WRONG?" I looked at Bruce who kept shaking his head back and forth, and I said, "Fucking shoot me now."

Heartbreaking? You'd better believe it was heartbreaking. I felt so guilty; I can't even describe the guilt that I felt. It hung from me like a weight. When I called him, I was SO sorry that I had done something so stupid and didn't even realize what the consequences would be. That poor man was a nervous wreck, thousands of miles away and he couldn't figure out what had happened. Oh, my God. Jackson wherever you are now, I am STILL guilt-ridden over that one. You poor baby. He cried and cried when he heard my voice on the phone. He thought I'd been in an accident or something else as terrible had happened and he had tried calling Frank and couldn't get him on the phone. He had to deal with the time difference and wait before he could call again, etc. It was a nightmare for that poor guy. You know, I kept that tape for years, because I was overwhelmed by the simple fact that someone would love me that much. When his daughter was older, we were talking about her father and I said to her, "You want to know what loving someone really is? Listen." And, I played the tape for her. What Is This Crazy Thing Called Love, huh??

People usually ask what it is like to live in another country. It is very exciting and very difficult. The excitement is in the obvious…that being, actually living in a totally different environment, 24-7 for God only knows how long. Jackson would criticize me for being "so American, you reek of it"; funny though because for that reason, I made friends as soon as I arrived. It was so exciting! The best thing to do is to not think about it until you get there. I never thought of how different it would be or I probably would not have gone. But, it is very, very different living in a foreign country. I know; such a vague statement. Right down to the basics, totally different. My day consisted of getting up at 4:30 a.m. to boil enough water for Jackson to bathe before leaving for work. I know. The French smell. They laugh at us because we bathe every day. And their teeth! Anyway, back to the boiling water.

Speaking of Jackson's travels, I would eventually join him in France, spending three months at a time with him, coming home and working for a few months and going back. It was a hectic schedule, but I enjoyed it. My mother was living in Pennsylvania with my sisters and my health had not exploded at that point.

We had an apartment in the old city and because of this being in an old building, our water heater was the size of a small coffee can. So, in five minutes, no hot water. Being the loyal partner that I am, I would get up and boil pots and pots of water to fill half of the tub and saved some so Jackson could shave. While he was getting ready, I would iron his shirt, start the coffee and his eggs. For toast, on went the oven and in went the buttered bread. The best toast I've ever eaten. Sometimes, I'd slice potatoes very thin and deep fry them, usually if he wanted scrambled eggs, and fry some ham. I would try my hardest to make it seem "southern." Jackson was not a big breakfast eater, so I had to make it to his liking. I always figured the smells of breakfast would anchor him to that table faster than my company. And, the coffee had to be good and strong. Once he was off and running, my day was basically the same, Monday through Friday. I would clean the kitchen from the breakfast mess and start my letters – a habit I developed when Jackson first moved to Europe was for me to sit down every morning (The time I missed him most) and write him a letter and also write in my journal. So, I kept up with this when I went to Europe. It took a couple hours for my letter writing which was accompanied by the morning sounds of the city. I would open the doors to the balcony off of the living room and while writing, I would listen to the traffic below and the people walking by. One difference between our country and many others is that foreigners tend to walk more on a daily basis than we do. We Americans are a spoiled lot. The 7/11 may be only a block away, but we will still drive to it. I did as the natives did and walked everywhere during the week. Once letters were written, to the post office. Now, you would think that in four years, I would have learned something of the language. Not a verb! I would tell Jackson where I had to go the next day and he would write out any questions I would have to ask. I would memorize it and carry it with me in case I destroyed the pronunciation which happened more often than not. However, one thing about the French, if you at least attempt to speak their language, they appreciate so much the gesture that they would start speaking English to me. The French are an odd group, rather moody most of the time. Their overall temperament usually reminded me of the personality of a cat. And so, I treated them the same way I treated my cat. I ignored them instead of trying to win their favor and would let them come to me and seek me out. What always upset Jackson was that people would come up to me and start rambling off, thinking I was French, and totally ignoring him thinking he was German or Scandinavian, because of the blonde hair and blue eyes.

I remember one night being in a gay bar not far from our apartment and sitting at a table talking quietly, when this very attractive man pulled a chair up next to me and started talking to me. Having no idea what he was saying, I asked Jackson to translate which he did and not happily, as the conversation progressed. Eventually, the man (who never looked at Jackson all the while he was translating) asked if I wanted to go to his apartment. At that point, Jackson snapped the stem of his martini glass right in half. In perfect English, the man said to Jackson, "Who are you?" To which Jackson replied, "I pay the bills!!" Shortly after that we left and I had to walk behind a very upset Jackson, apologizing all the way home. Gosh, I was always apologizing for something while we lived in France, but I was never quite sure why.

There is a wonderful park up the street from our apartment and I would usually buy a sandwich and bottled water, and head there for lunch with either the English newspaper or a book I would purchase at the book shop which was run by two women from England. I read everything ever written by Agatha Christie – twice. I would go to the park because they had swans there and I would have my lunch and the swans would be my "guests" for the afternoon. The only outings with Jackson took place on the weekends. We would head out into the countryside and explore. We would look for cathedral steeples off in the distance and decide if we wanted to stop in that particular village and see what the rest of the church had to offer. They were usually very old and very beautiful, and in the country the people were always very friendly and helpful, as to good local restaurants or where to get gas, etc. If we did stop, I would walk up to the front of the church and hit the pavement at the front steps to take pictures of the steeples. Usually, I couldn't get a picture of the entire church and one day I decided to stretch out, prone on my back with tourists trying to walk around me or over me, but I got the shot I wanted. Two steeples with church centered in the snapshot. Not bad. Jackson used to walk away from me as I would go down. Wonderful memories, too.

During the summers, when his daughter would come over for her vacation from school, she and I would drive out to the coast and stretch out on the beach and bake. During the week, we would drive Jackson to work and head out to the beach ourselves, not knowing a word of French between us or how crazy the driving could be in a foreign country, but off we would go and have a ball together. We would talk for hours or go for walks together through the old city. What a thrill to see history – to walk down the street and touch walls where the Nazi's bullets had grazed the buildings or to see a cathedral Claude Monet painted in a series of portraits. The thrill of actually being there and seeing structures from the 11th and 12th centuries. Incredible.

As I said, I never learned to speak French; however, I discovered that if immersed totally in a culture with nowhere else to go, and all you see and hear is another language everywhere you go; on the radio, on television; the music, art, everything, you slowly begin to understand the language because you begin to understand what the gestures indicate, what the person's tone infers. At first, it will be a word, a phrase. You find that you can string the words and phrases together – et voila! Suddenly, you understand! You still cannot answer them, but you know what they said to you. At first, I didn't let on to Jackson. One night while having dinner with friends, I was listening to the conversation and started laughing at what our friend Philippe had said. The secret was out. Everyone looked at me and started laughing out of surprise. So many of them are now dead, but live on in my memories. Their lovely voices and charming smiles; their laughter especially. Always the laughter of a group of friends sharing dinner, wine and conversation, are the best and brightest memories for me, and many nights both in America and France, were spent with friends. Sometimes I believe that my friends are literally the air I breathe for they make living possible for me. Why live if you cannot surround yourself with people you love and love being with? How I miss them, especially those that have died. Several years after leaving France, three of our friends in France came for a visit and brought friends with them from NYC to visit us in Massachusetts. Thank God for five bedrooms! Our home seemed to come alive when filled to capacity. Holidays loaded with guests were heaven in our house because it was so spacious. You never felt crowded. Anyone at any time could go off to any corner of the house or to a study or out into the garden and just be. It was a wonderful house and I loved it. I enjoyed nothing as much as fixing it up or painting a room or hallway to spruce it up, or decorate it for the holidays. These were my moments of bonding with our home. I felt as if I knew it, knew its rhythm, its strengths and weaknesses, and I wanted to stay there and take care of it, love it and bring it back to its former glory. I used to tell people that having moved so often, I had finally found a place to call home and I'd leave there in a body bag and it would be the only way they would get me out. I came pretty damn close a couple of times, but life had other things in store for me. Odd, but my years there were the happiest of my life. Thank you, dear house, for loving me in return and making me feel safe and welcome. Actually, I should take the time now to tell you something about our home and our life together in Massachusetts. Then, I'll get back to the main story. This is how my life has been lived as well; sort of scattered, jumping from place to place. I hope you don't find keeping up with my thoughts too confusing. An impression I wish to leave with you is how confusing my life was.

We had two months left on our lease and we decided to wait it out for the time being. That gave me time to focus on my mother. She was at a point where she was very quiet. The Alzheimer's had affected her ability to initiate a conversation and she would also mimic your statements. It is called "parroting"; much like teaching a parrot different phrases and having it repeat them back to you. I felt that there was so much going on in my life at the time that I needed my sisters to help temporarily. Now came the time to start packing everything and putting it all in storage until we found a place of our own in Massachusetts. At the end of the first month left of our lease in Rochester, I was feeling fit and back to normal, which meant I had enough energy to do what had to be done.

For now, it was really nice and felt very similar to the beginning of our relationship. I took a hiatus from working and focused totally on building our life in New England and keeping an eye on my mother while she was still in Pennsylvania. As was my style, by the time everything was completed in Rochester, I had already begun contacting real-estate agents to set up appointments to scout out possible buys in and around central Massachusetts.

With his work schedule, we focused mainly on weekend outings or, if it was important, I would meet the agent, scout out the property and tell Jackson what I thought and/or if we both needed to take a second look at it. That really did save time in the end for us and was less stressful for Jackson. This went on every weekend for two months. We saw some beautiful homes in very picturesque surroundings; very "New England" looking with ties to colonial times or one-family ownership for four generations. These sorts of things were used to jack up the asking price to almost double its market value. One odd thing I noticed about living in Massachusetts, a relatively small state, is that everyone is super aware of where you live and how far it is from Boston. It seemed that if you didn't live in Boston, you didn't live in

Massachusetts. Outside of Boston and the first ring of suburbs, and you lived in the "country." Such snobs. And, all over a piece of land.

One Saturday afternoon in early October, we met with an agent I had contacted during the week to see an old colonial house in a small town outside of Worcester. We went, hoping that this was "the house", our home. Arriving there, we saw a beautiful Greek Revival style house; however, the back yard had been sold to build a high-rise complex for senior citizens. The front yard faced a traffic circle. Now, who wouldn't want to buy this little piece of history? And, as it was, they were asking almost $200,000.00 Jackson stood there, staring at me. I knew what he was thinking. So, before he exploded, I asked the agent if there was anything else that she had in mind. She said that there was a house that she knew of that had been on the market for a while, but it wasn't a colonial or federal-period house. But, if we wanted to see it, it was not far from where we were; actually, the next town over. We figured we had nothing to lose. We were already there, so why not. Odd as it sounds, I told Jackson during the drive that I had had it with looking at houses and this one was the last for me. He agreed and said we would take a break after we saw this house. We were tired of trekking all over central Massachusetts, looking at places that had almost nothing in common with the description we had given the agent. We soon realized that most agents were interested in showing properties to make a sale. It can be very frustrating to try and be so specific in your description, thinking you're saving them time and energy, only to have them drag you 20-30 minutes out into the country to show you a Victorian "painted lady" complete with wrap-around porch and original carriage house, when you told them you were looking for a 1700's colonial, or a stone farmhouse, or a Greek Revival, or a cobblestone house, which is a rarity to find for sale. But, off we went, interested in what the agent thought we might want to see.

Taking route 2 west, we followed the agent, getting off at a town named Gardner. This was in October which is an incredible time of year in New England. Visually, unbelievable experiences as the autumn colors are so striking at that time. Actually, we were to discover later that people come from all over the country for the fall foliage in New England. We got off the highway and drove past a shopping plaza, up the boulevard and past the high school. When you reach the high school, there is a huge, three-story-in-height chair in front of the school. We learned that Gardner was known as the "Chair City" because it had been a center for furniture manufacturing. Interestingly, many towns in central Massachusetts have nicknames that designate their industrial history.

We arrived to view a monstrous Tudor-Revival house which was a very popular style in the 1920's and early 1930's in America. We waited at the front door while the agent went to the back door and the lock box. As we waited, we looked at the yard which was somewhat in disarray. Apparently, the owners were into "natural" landscaping which means there were no flowers except for a row of rhododendron in the front of the house that were so overgrown they covered the front windows of the house. As the house was on a corner lot, the other street side had an overgrown evergreen hedge that also blocked any view of the ground floor. What you couldn't see was the beautiful brick work that covered the entire ground floor of the house and the bushes gave the house a very dark and dreary appearance. Scanning the second and third floors, I could see that the house was in desperate need of a paint job on the stucco element and there were also parts of the original copper gutters that were missing. I also noticed a beautiful but very steep-pitched slate roof, and chimneys that needed work as well. By this time, the agent was at the front door and letting us in to the foyer and into the entry hallway. As soon as we entered, I knew that the house was haunted. You could feel a level of energy pulsating under the surface. I immediately asked the agent if the house was haunted. As quickly, Jackson gave me a penetrating look as we waited for her reply which was "Not that I am aware." That intrigued me, as well as the fact that she never looked at us when she answered and she kept on walking as she did answer my question. There was also something in her voice that made me think twice about her reply. As she and Jackson meandered through the empty rooms downstairs, making their way to the dining room and kitchen, I held back and waited. When I realized they had gone on, I closed my eyes and began breathing deeply and relaxing. Once I opened up and sought it out, I could feel the source of energy I described earlier. It ran like a current under the surface of the space within the house. The difference that I felt was that it was following us, tracking us, wondering almost who we were and what we were doing there, which also made me realize that it had a certain level of intelligence. Now this I found fascinating. After a few minutes, Jackson called for me and I opened my eyes and closed down to a normal energy level and caught up with them as they were going up the back stairway to the second floor. As I approached, Jackson asked inquisitively, "And, what IS going on with you, J?" "Nothing at all. I'm taking in the house on different levels." Jackson was like my mother and did not want to know about my psychic experiences, which scared him. I remember thinking as we walked through the upstairs that this poor house had been so neglected over the years and it was time that someone gave something back to it, so it could continue.

The house was huge! According to the agent, the owners had moved to California over a year ago and it had been left unoccupied all that time. Originally, they were asking $200,000.00 for it and no one was interested. It was the "gem" on the realtor's list, but the area could not support that price range – too far from Boston to have an impact on the price of real estate.

As for the physical presence of the house, downstairs consisted of the entry way which led to a four-tiered main stairway to the right, facing the front doors. To the left was a huge (18 x 28) living room with fireplace and bookshelves. Off of this was a study with another fireplace and a door leading to the side yard. Straight ahead you walked past a small privy under the main stairway. Beyond that was a huge (16 x 20) dining room with a window seat the length of the banquet of windows at the end of the room. From there, you walked through a butler's pantry to the kitchen. Also, off the pantry was a smaller room that was used for informal, daily meals. The cellar door and door to the back stairway, as well as the rear entrance from the driveway, all converged here, in the pantry. So many doors in one place! It always confused people when they were in that part of the house as to which door went where. And, there were 65 windows in total! That's a lot of Windex! As we climbed the back stairs, we came upon the back bedroom which had its own dressing room, built-in closets and drawers, and its own bathroom. To the side of the bathroom door, the stairway continued to the third floor, which had two bedrooms and full bathroom, and attic space. On the second floor, we continued to the left and down the hall leading to the front of the house. Along the hall and under the third-floor stairway was a small closet which contained the laundry chute. At the front of the house there was the master bedroom with its own study with fireplace and bookshelves, private bathroom and dressing room with built-in closets and drawers. Across from this was a smaller guest bedroom and in the corner of the house at the top of the main stairway was a room which had been used as a nursery, complete with built-in window seat and dormer windows because of the steep pitch of the roof in this part of the house. I loved it. I thought it was perfect and fell in love with the house as soon as we walked in. True, it needed a lot of work, but it was worth it and I was willing to do it. Jackson took one look at me and said to the agent, "I'll make an offer of $145,000.00 for it." Surprised that we were that interested so soon, she asked if we were sure. We said that we were and she told us that the price had come down considerably in the time the house had been on the market, down to $155,000.00. Jackson said, "Yes, but it needs a lot of work, especially after sitting empty through an entire winter. It is now October. Empty another winter and they will have to give it away. My offer stands." I wanted to deck him, thinking we would lose it. Once in the car, he reminded me that these people were in California. They did not want to come back to take care of the property. It had already been over a year and no one was interested, even though they had come down almost $50,000.00 in the price and they knew that another six months of heating bills would probably break them, as they couldn't afford two mortgages for much longer. What a shrew. I would have never thought of any of that. I have never had that killer instinct. Like sharks when the scent of blood is in the water. A week later, they accepted the offer.

By the end of October, we were in. Once the furniture arrived and everything was set in place, we went to Pennsylvania to collect my mother. A sad moment. When she saw the house, she loved it, but kept asking us who owned it. It was sad for me because it was the type of home she would have loved; spacious, six bedrooms, 3 fireplaces, and an older home. She was not crazy about new. Like me, she was attracted to something with character and history. It was the last home she would know to any degree, but that was yet to come. For the moment, Jackson and I were caught up in the excitement of owning and furnishing our home. The hardest part was the living room. It was so large that eventually it held three sofas and two conversation areas consisting of two wing-back chairs plus six end/coffee tables and lamps and a huge oriental rug that had been Jackson's grandmother's. It really was beautiful. I used to keep shear panels on the windows and our neighbors said they loved walking by in the evening and looking in because I would turn on all of the antique Tiffany lamps in the living room and the room shone.

Also, from the moment we did move in, the spirits let us know they were there. Most of the time they left Jackson alone. However, because I was sensitive and open to them, they had a field day with me and our cats. Sometimes, my dog Missie, would be alone in a room and bark at nothing I could see, or she and I would be in the study or living room while I was reading and she would perk up and start growling. The cats? Well, that was another story. The spirits loved teasing our cats. But, I'll start at the beginning.

The day after my mom arrived, the spirits decided to kick in and welcome her. Jackson had left for work and mom and I were unpacking dishes in the kitchen. All of a sudden, there was this very loud and distinctive sound of glass hitting the dining room floor and shattering. I ran in to the dining room to see what had happened --- nothing. The boxes were where we had left them, the chandelier was still intact suspended from the ceiling above the table. Nothing had happened, yet I knew what I had heard. This happened three or four times until finally my mother said, "You have spooks in this house." When Jackson came home that night I told him of the day's events and he looked at mom and she shook her head in the affirmative and said, "Spooks." Yes, we had spooks. In the plural, too. I noticed that there was an entirely different level of energy downstairs than what I felt on the third floor. To me, very little seemed to be happening on the second floor. There were strange occurrences over the years that were experienced by us, as well as by other people; strangers and family.

On the one occasion that my family came to visit for a holiday, I have to admit that the spirits did not take to my older sister at all. They walked behind her, she felt someone's breath on her neck, the TV turned on by itself in our study one day while she was in there, reading. They would not leave her alone. The worst was one night while we were all in the study talking, she came running down the hallway screaming that something kept turning the light on and off while she was in the bathroom off the back bedroom. That night at about 2:00 a.m., my niece woke everyone with her screams because she was awakened by the sound of her baby who was in the playpen wide awake, giggling at something and what made my niece scream was when she realized that some "thing" wound up the musical carousel that was suspended from the side of the playpen and it started moving and playing music. Someone had to wind it up and only she and the baby were in the bedroom. She switched rooms with her cousin that night. My God, in the six years I lived there, the experiences were incredible, but I always felt safe there and protected by whatever was there. From pictures coming off the walls and landing on the floor, to lights going on and off, to candles being blown out, to hearing footsteps going up the main stairway every night at 11:00 p.m. sharp, to jewelry appearing on the floor and charred bits of paper that were time tested to being 100 years old, to seeing apparitions of complete bodies to an apparition one day of a pair of legs walking down the main stairway, to candlesticks coming off of the mantel in the living room and being dragged toward me and my cat Sandy, to seeing puffs of smoke and orbs of light sailing through the air, to birds flying into the windows and knocking themselves unconscious, to moving cold spots, to séances and TV crews from Hollywood and Boston, to hearing crying during the night and a dog scratching and barking at the back door and when you opened it nothing was there. We had it all. It was the most exciting time of my life, but the most terrifying for Jackson. That poor guy. He was absolutely terrified to be in that house alone. When he was home, I couldn't move. I was in for the night. Yet, none of it ever bothered me. I felt as if I had finally found my element. I had been tested in college and told that I was precognitive, which I already knew from the dreams I had had for most of my life. I dreamt about relatives who were ill, who were to have surgery, accidents. The worst were the dreams of relatives dying. I hated those. They were actually the reason I decided to block the dreams and impressions, and until I moved to Massachusetts, I totally ignored them. Once we moved into our home, I knew that it was time to open up again, as it would help me. I know how people tend to feel about Ouija® boards. Personally, I've never had a bad experience when using them. I can't verify what the board told us, but I can relay what happened that night.

Our first winter there a friend from Philadelphia came to visit. He brought with him a Ouija® board. As it happened, Jackson was in Europe on business. Jeff and I had known each other for many years and hadn't seen each other in quite a while. So, we had decided to relax for the long weekend he was going to visit. I drove in to the train station and picked him up. The weather forecast for the weekend was very foreboding. Our first winter in Massachusetts it snowed every day for almost 30 days. I had never seen anything like it in my life. It never seemed to stop.

On Thursday night the snow did let up, briefly. The sky was as always, a permanent drab gray with the constant threat of snow, snow and…snow. I picked up Jeff around 10:00 p.m., as there had been delays during the train's slow trek northeast from Philadelphia. Jeff was exhausted and cold upon the train's arrival in Worcester. It was a slow trek for us to get home as well, but we made it. I got Jeff situated and while he unpacked and changed, I ran him a hot bath so he could warm up and unwind. As he settled into the warm water and steamy bathroom, I lit a fire in our study's fireplace upstairs and relaxed, watching it begin again to snow. Jeff and I sat up and talked well into the early morning, until we were both running on empty and tired of watching it snow. Later that morning, my day began with shoveling the driveway and starting the first pot of coffee of the day. Shortly, I could hear Jeff stirring upstairs, knowing the scent of coffee would open his eyes, and the need for a cigarette. About 15 minutes later, there stood Jeff in the kitchen in his old robe, cigarette in tow. "You are really enjoying this 'New England' life, aren't you?" was his opening line for the day. I laughed. "Yes, I am, smartass. Now, do you want anything solid for breakfast?" "What's the house special?" was his comment, as he dragged himself to the fridge scratching his stomach, to survey the bounty. We had breakfast in the dining room and were struck by the incredible amount of snow that kept falling and falling. Jeff was relieved to have finally made it. He told me the weather had been horrible the entire trip but worst once they passed into New England. I told him that a storm pattern was stuck over New England and kept pulling moisture in from the Atlantic and Canada and would keep dumping snow until another front came in that was strong enough to push this one out over the Atlantic. It was so peaceful though to sit in the house and watch it snow. I saw very few people outside, neighbors shoveling basically nonstop. The previous week I had shopped enough for two months' worth of nonstop snowfall. So, we were safe. The problem became electricity. It was beginning to flicker on Saturday, so we weren't sure how long it would last. However, I'd pulled in plenty of wood for the fireplaces and stacked candles and oil lamps all through the house. We were safe there, too. Jackson had phoned Friday night, saying that he was stuck in London due to the weather and was not sure when he would be home. Well, at least I knew that he was safe and on dry land.

Jeff proposed that since we were to be housebound, why not use the Ouija® board tonight. "Sounds good to me," I shouted, "but let me take one more shot at the driveway and we'll have a late lunch." We spent the early part of the evening catching up on old friends, Jeff's life in Philadelphia and my life with Jackson, as he and Jeff were yet to meet.

I was in the kitchen making more coffee to save in case of a blackout, when Jeff suggested 10:00 p.m. as a good time for the Ouija® board. That would give me some time to get things situated in case the storm really kicked into high gear for the night ahead. Once the animals were set up with food and fresh water and litter, and the dog had been out trying to find a spot to relieve herself and having success, I brought her in and once again checked the candles and lamps, made another pot of coffee for Jeff and filled another thermos which I figured was enough to get us through the night. I went upstairs and secured comforters and pillows for us, a flashlight for emergencies, and made sure that all of the windows upstairs were secured and closed doors to all the rooms on the second and third floors that weren't being used to cut down on the space being heated. Since it had not stopped snowing and the winds were picking up, I knew that we weren't going anywhere as the weather was kicking up to Nor'easter standards. It would turn into one of the stranger experiences I've known in my life.

Once we agreed on the time to start, you could feel the energy stir in the atmosphere of the house, as if in anticipation of their opportunity to finally "talk". Jeff is sensitive as well and agreed about the feeling of anticipation building. The air became almost electric as the time grew nearer. As well, the storm outside was growing in intensity. The winds were becoming fierce, along with bands of heavy snow which continued to fall. It was getting scary.

By 9:30, we were without power. Jeff and I already had fires going in the living room and study. We wrapped ourselves in comforters and squatted on the floor in front of the living room fireplace. With the wind howling all around us and the snow coming fast and furious, we began our journey. Our friendship would never be the same after that night spent together in front of the glow and warmth of that fire. The intensity of the moment was as strong that night in that living room as it was outside the house in the storm of the decade that seemed to want "in," as well.

I stood to light the candles on the mantel and walked into the study to light more candles. As I came back into the living room and lighted the antique oil lamp in the front window, I heard Jeff whisper, "J, we're not alone." As I turned to answer him, I saw that one candle on the mantel had gone out and the second was blown out as I looked at it. Watching the smoke swirl up from the candles, Jeff turned toward me with this look of "Oh, shit!!" on his face and I said, "See Jeff. I told you we'd have fun tonight." I took a deep breath to steady my hands and lit candles on the side tables, re-lit those on the mantel and sat back down so we could get to work. Jeff had stocked himself up with a thermos of coffee and several packs of cigarettes. "If only the damn winds would die down, it wouldn't seem so eerie." Poor Jeff. He was stuck now and beginning to realize that fact, and there was nowhere to run. As the clock on the mantel chimed 10, we broke out the board and began.

There was an immediate response and very strong. We knew that it was a male presence. As it turned out, there were several spirits present, all wanting to talk with us. The story that we were given was that they were a group traveling by coach from Montreal to Boston and this part of the journey involved an old Indian trail. They had decided to camp overnight on what would become our property and were robbed and murdered by "rogues," as they called them, found by Indians and buried in the "NW corner of your land under the big, old tree, where no grass grows." This was true. There was a bald spot in the corner of the front yard in the shape of a body. The previous owners said no matter what they tried nothing would grow there. I had also spoken with an older couple, who owned the home for many years during the 1950s through the 1970s and they told me the same story. I guess now we knew why nothing grew there. The only way that I can describe our session that night is to say that it was extremely enlightening for me. Men and women came through and you could always tell the difference by the weight and power being used to move the indicator on the board. Actually, one woman came through, a governess, who spoke only French. So, we wrote down her message for Jackson, fluent in French, to translate when he came home. It was fascinating. They told us that they could see us, but it was like looking through a thin sheet of water. Also, they were drawn to me because I would sing around the house and one spirit said that he followed me because my laughter was energetic, "like life itself," as he put it. They told us of the colors of our auras and that they were drawn to us when Jackson and I were making love because of the bright white light that our energy created around us. They told us that they left periodically to "go to our source and 're-energize'" (I never quite understood that one). They also told us of our great epidemic (AIDS) and that a cure would be found. Also, that a major war was coming but rather than heavy casualties that there would be mass enslavement. It went on and on in this vein. I was totally absorbed in the reading and taking notes that we could study afterward. Poor Jeff begged that we take a break to get up and stretch and go to the bathroom. To my amazement almost three hours had passed. In the kitchen, Jeff was telling me that he was having a difficult time accepting what was happening; the number of spirits, their distinct personality differences coming through the board, their individual messages, plus what they had told us about the future. I felt and told him that he was trying to absorb too much at once. Plus the elements heightening everything around us; the constant roar of the wind and snow battering the house, the electricity going out and the feeling of anticipation palpably building throughout the day, up to the moment we sat down. I told him that we needed to document tonight, leave it alone and go back and check it after a mental break from it. He was a little hesitant, smoking way too much, but agreed.

We went back to the living room and sat at the board and I asked them when my partner would be home, as I was concerned about his flying in this weather. The spirits said, "Sooner than you think." I no sooner had their answer written down when we heard a car pull into the driveway and there was Jackson! That really put Jeff over the edge and he refused to go back to the board after that. I was so relieved to see Jackson. The weather was horrific and I couldn't believe that he had actually found a limo to rent that would drive through this storm. Hugging me and catching his breath while brushing snow from his overcoat, he told me, "I offered double the usual rate and suddenly the storm didn't seem so awful to the driver". However, he told us that because of the storm, it took almost three hours to reach home from Logan, which is usually no more than an hour's drive. I didn't care. I was so happy to see him, safe.

I introduced Jackson to Jeff, told him about the power outage, and what we had been doing. Before he became terrified, I informed him that there was a message for him, but that he had to translate it as it came through in French. Now this he found intriguing enough to overcome his fear. Candle in hand, he went upstairs and changed into warmer clothes, the heat being gone since the outage, grabbed a comforter and joined us in the living room. By now, Jeff had had enough and watched, as Jackson translated the message left for him. Jackson looked at the notes and said, "Oh, this is in old French". Suddenly, he stood up, dropped the notes and said, "Put it away!" Jeff and I exchanged glances and I noted that Jackson's eyes had welled up with tears. "Jackson, are you all right?", I asked. As he tore up the notes from the board, he kept repeating, "Put it away! Just put it away," and threw the scraps into the fire. He announced that he was very tired and was going to bed, leaving the room as he spoke to us. "Jackson, what's wrong?", I again asked. Looking over at Jeff, I couldn't figure out what had happened to him. Damn! I wish I understood old French! I told Jeff that I was heading upstairs to see what was going on. I told him not to worry about the fires that they would burn out and I would take care of everything in the morning. He jumped up and his eyes widened. "You're not leaving me down here all alone! After what's happened? I'm coming, too!" So, like Lucy and Ethel, up the stairs we crept, tripping over one another as I blew out what was left of the candles.

Once upstairs and in bed, listening to the force of the wind as it hit the house in the night, I reached for Jackson and asked again if he was okay. Without turning toward me, he said quietly, "I'm sorry if I upset Jeff, but I didn't want to discuss it. Turning over onto his back, he continued, "It was a message from my mother about an incident that took place when I was a teenager. It involved my mother, no one else. There is no way either of you could have known about it. Even I haven't thought about it in years. I wasn't here when it was given to you, so there's no way I impacted upon the message. I can only believe that it really was a message for me from her. I don't want to discuss it, ever, J. Ever". To this day, I have no idea what that message held for Jackson. I never again questioned him about it. What I discovered was that this was how he dealt with any kind of upsetting news. It disappeared, did not exist; my illness, my mother's illness and death, his affairs. Anything that showed a weakness, a vulnerability on his part did not happen. Work for Jackson became the balm. And I ceded to his wishes to try and keep the peace.

Believe it or not, there finally came a break in our cycle-of-snow weather. The next morning, the sun shone, the winds and snowfall were gone and it was a crystal-clear sky. I woke early as usual and dressed to go outside and check for damage. Some time during the night our power returned so I ran around re-setting clocks, getting the coffee going, checking for heat and hot water, feeding the dog and cats. I threw on boots and headed out. What a sight. There were drifts against the house up to the second floor windows. The driveway was a memory as the wind blew the snow to the lilac hedge that ran along the drive and piled the snow between the back of the house and the hedgerow blocking the way to the garage, to the side yard, to the road. My passage was totally cut off since the snow buried the back porch as well. Winter in New England! I had to go out through the study door into the side yard and start tunneling my way to the back porch. Once I found the porch, I started on where I thought I had parked the car in the drive. An hour later I finally had the car cleared and a path to the back door completed. Enough! I needed a break. In I went through the back door and dropped my frozen coat, hat, gloves and boots all in the mud room before entering the pantry and kitchen. The cats now enveloped the radiator in the kitchen that sat under the back window and Jeff was walking around above me in the back bedroom, roused by the coffee from his state of hibernation underneath the mountain of blankets and comforters he had created to stay warm through the night. I poured coffee and decided to head into the living room to try and piece last night together again in the light of the new day.

The only bump in the road I could see was Jackson's unexpected reaction to his message. As I cleaned out the fireplaces and collected comforters and candles, I re-ran the memory of events from last night and really was amazed at how a simple event became somewhat monumental. I began seeing the events as a series of moments linked together, culminating in Jackson's moment from Hell and I wondered if the entire night was used to create some sort of illusion and diversion for Jeff and myself with the real reason for the event being to get that message to Jackson from his mother. Now, I was stumped because of his refusal to discuss what had taken place.

Jeff was never quite the same after that visit. I wrote, called and e-mailed, but it was almost two years before I heard again from him. When he did write, he told me that he felt that something had followed him home because strange things began to happen in Philadelphia. The day after returning home, his car was totaled at an intersection a block from his house. The night he arrived home, he opened the door to his house and found a set of old skeleton keys on the floor inside the front door, sitting on the floor, as if to make sure he would see them as soon as he came home. They weren't his. He had no idea where they had come from. The day of the accident, he started receiving dead phone calls. He would hear his name and the line would go dead. When it was traced, it was listed as out of area. So, he began to freak over the whole situation and decided to leave it all alone until things settled down. I was surprised by all of this and had to remind him that bringing the board was his idea, not mine, and that he left the board at my house so I wasn't sure how he brought anything back to Philadelphia with him, but I accepted his explanation and was glad to know that he was all right.

In reality, I was to never know the truth of that evening, but I have always been haunted by it. Living there was an incredible experience for me and many major events of my life took place while living in that wonderful, old house. The house had been on television twice; once, a national show was interested in filming there with a crew of parapsychologists. That was different! Two days of the house being torn up with huge lights everywhere and wires. It was proven to be an authentic haunting, though. The one parapsychologist said that it was a classic haunting, in that the entities moved around and followed us. The other show was a Boston TV channel that had called to ask if they could bring a British psychic to the house. Apparently, she had somehow heard about the house and wanted to "experience" it, too. Out they came! She was very nice and very gifted. Knew my name, as I recall, before our being introduced AND the name of a friend of mine who was visiting from Rochester. There was no way she could have known my friend's name. She walked through the house with the producer while I walked behind them. As she said things, the producer would look back at me and I was to shake my head either in the affirmative or negative at her comments. She hit absolutely everything, including my mother's death and how she died. I was absolutely floored. She really was incredible. Almost as incredible as the house itself. Whatever was there had an instinct of its own and that is what scared people the most when they experienced something, because it usually was something out of the ordinary, but specific to that person. The entity always somehow made it personal. I believe that is what people found terrifying.

I also think that I viewed the house as a living thing, an extension of our relationship. There are two periods of time in my life that I would re-live; the time I spent with Dell and the time I spent in that house in Massachusetts. Now, that's odd, isn't it. I didn't say "the time I spent with Jackson". Hmm... Well, now back to the story.

Chapter Five

"Like I've quietly lost my life.
It's the awareness of that" -
"Love Warps the Mind a Little,"
by John DuFresne

O ne day a relative came to our house for a visit when I was
about 10. He was 15. I was the only one at home. He came
into my bedroom and closed the door and told me he had
something to show me. He exposed himself to me. An alarm
went off, but I wasn't quite sure why. After all, he WAS a
relative. Why should I be afraid of him? He took my hand and
told me to hold his erection. I pulled back and the next thing I
knew he was on top of me on my bed, pulling down my pants.
Very quickly, he rolled me over onto my stomach and I
remember him putting his elbow into the back of my neck to keep
my head down and holding my hands with one of his. He had
straddled the backs of my knees with his and then there was the
most intense pain I've probably ever known as he penetrated me.
It didn't take long, but the emotional scars have lasted my entire
life. I remember that he got up and left, threatening to kill me if I
ever told anyone. I was 10 and wanted to see 11. I don't know
how long I lay there consumed by the pain and pressure I felt in
my butt. Not knowing IF I could move or if I should even try. I

felt something wet, and I went into the bathroom to discover that I was bleeding. Or, had bled. Actually, by that time it had stopped. But still, there was blood on the toilet paper. I don't know why, but I thought it would be a good idea to take a bath. That comes from having a mother who was a nurse. In times of emergency, scrub. Oh my God. When I sat in that tub, what pain. But, eventually it did help. And, I never told anyone. It went on for almost two years, until one day when I came home from school, went upstairs, and found that same relative in bed with my father, having oral sex. Thanks to that relative, I knew exactly what they were doing and what those sounds meant. Over the years I have wondered at times what it must have felt like for this relative, to know that he had taken the son and had the father. There seems to be something almost biblical in that scenario. However, that ended my relative's attacks on me, but my father started beating me, I think because he was afraid I would tell. I never did. I couldn't tell my mother. I couldn't. I think now that I never said anything to anyone because I never felt that there was anyone I could tell. When I finally told my sister about it a year ago, her first response was, "Why didn't you tell us?" I said, "Tell you? All of you were abusive to me. Who was there that I could trust enough to tell? I had no one." I had an escape mechanism I used as a kid; a field where I would go to escape the abuse at home. I think at some point in my childhood, during some form of abuse, I mentally went to that spot in the field and I never came back until many years later. I think that I lived on automatic pilot so no one could ever hurt me again, that I would feel. However, what I didn't know at the time was that this relative of mine had exposed me to the hepatitis B virus and it would lay dormant for many years, eating away at my liver, almost destroying it and killing me. That was the legacy I was left with after that hot summer's day when I was 10 years old and my life took a sharp turn. Many years later, I met Jackson, and I came back into living my life. Believe me, it was the worst mistake I could have made. He devastated me in ways no one could have thought possible. But after he left, instead of retreating back into myself, I was older at that point and chose to continue living my life and finding the answers to my life's questions. Thus, this story. Does this help you to understand any better why I would stay in a relationship with him for almost 11 years and not find what he did to be abusive? He didn't throw me into a closet. He didn't rape me. He didn't beat me. Where was the abuse? What a fool, but I learned.

You have to understand that I found love to be a scary thing. I could never quite trust it when it came into my life. My father was the type of man who felt it necessary to be tough with me, so that I'd be "ready" for life. Yea, one of those. When I was a child, my father would lock me in a closet for punishment and I couldn't make a sound or I'd get hauled out, beaten again and put back into the closet. There was a field not far from our house and when I was a kid, I used to ride my bike there and sit for hours in a spot I'd picked out and read or watch the sky, listening to the birds. Anyway, when I was put into that closet, I'd "go" to my spot there in the field, and forget that I was actually sitting in the dark in a closet, and it would calm me. When I was a child, my father would take me for rides downtown and drop me off on a corner, telling me to find my way home. For years and years afterward, whenever I got into a car someone else was driving, out of habit, I would "spot" buildings so I'd remember the way back home. It used to drive my first lover, Dell, absolutely wild. I wasn't even aware that I was still doing it until he pulled over one day while we were out and asked me what the hell I was doing. I knew that I still carried it with me. When I was a child, for punishment, my father would lock me out on a side porch of our house and I would have to stand there, watching him and my sisters eating dinner, summer or winter. When I was a child, my father would play what he called, "Irish Roulette," when he was drunk. He would take me in the car for a ride that went usually with his foot on the gas pedal hitting about 80 MPH, riding other people's bumpers and not stopping for stop signs or red lights, seeing how long his luck would hold out, and I couldn't make a sound. No, that was a sign of weakness. And, God forbid he should see that I had closed my eyes. That meant a stint in the closet when we got back home. No, you sat there, watched, and did all of your screaming inside of your head. When I was a child, I used to hide in the bushes in our neighborhood when my mother was at work, because my father would get drunk and get in the car and do a "search" for me, cruising the neighborhood with his flashlight, looking for me to see if I was hiding in a neighbor's yard or under someone's porch. That would go on for hours, while my sisters watched TV or did their homework, until he grew tired and/or went home and passed out. It was then safe for me to sneak onto the roof of the back porch and come in through the bedroom window and go to sleep. If I was visiting at a relative's house, he'd barge in, grab me by the hand and drag me out of their house. When I was a child, I hauled ashes from the basement in the winter, shoveled snow from the sidewalks and driveway, mowed the lawn in the summer, raked leaves in the fall, and took out the garbage year-round. That's what a man did. Funny but I never remember my father, a man, doing any of it. Actually, he never held a job until he met my mother. She found a job for him where she worked, cleaning offices. A janitor. But, he was my father. More important, my mother was in love with him, so she was blind to a lot of what he was doing while she was at work. When I was a child, I can remember Christmases spent at the Salvation Army and Thanksgivings spent at the Salvation Army. I can remember walking along the train tracks picking coal to take home for the furnace, to stock up for winter. I can remember being on welfare, when there were no food stamps and you went to the railroad yards to get government-processed food. It wasn't the luxurious way-of-life it has become today. The idea was to get you off of welfare ASAP, and that was usually done through means of public humiliation. I can remember being in school and having the county nurse and/or doctor come in and take me out of class to an empty classroom and have me strip in front of my teacher, and be examined for bugs and lice, while they "chatted". You had no warning when they were coming to inspect you or your home. They just showed up, and everything had better have been clean. But, for me, it was the norm. I presumed that everyone lived like that. Actually, until my mother started working, it was in some ways a wonderful life because of its simplicity. Everything was homemade: bread, pasta, and sauce, fresh food cooked every day of the week. My mother always told us, we may be poor but that was no excuse to be dirty. We had little but what we had we took care of because we knew it had to last. To this day, you cannot use the word "needy" in front of my oldest sister. She goes ballistic. My mother started working, cleaning offices. I was a kid, but I went with her and helped. I have been working for as long as I can remember. If we weren't cleaning offices, we were cleaning houses. Relatives, friends, strangers. It didn't matter. If you wanted money for something, you had to earn it. We were poor but you never saw sheets hanging on our windows like you do today. Spring-cleaning was a major thing in our house. Blinds came down and were scrubbed in the tub and draped over the clothesline to dry. Floors and walls were scrubbed. You used a butter-knife with a washcloth wrapped around it for the baseboard grooves and door frames to get out all of the dirt. I use that one to this day, and it still works. You used newspaper and white vinegar for the windows. Mattresses were aired and pillows were draped over windowsills. Carpets were taken outside and beaten on the lawn and left to air. My mother missed nothing. You wiped down the rafters and the furnace in the basement. And, since dust settled, you started at the top and worked your way down. I can remember my mother using a wringer washing machine, holding the clothes as they were pressed through the two rollers to wring out the water. She'd never let me near that thing; afraid I'd crush a hand. Everything was starched with starch that had been boiled that morning. Everything that was to be ironed was dampened (My mother used the now-classic Coke bottle with the spritzer cork/metal top), rolled like cabbage rolls, and placed in the refrigerator until it was time to iron. I still say that was the best way to clean a house and iron clothing. Everything today looks so mussed or unmade. My older sister was famous for tearing everything apart and disappearing for the really hard work. She would always end up at my Aunt A's house. My mom would look at me and I'd do double-work. I think we accomplished more minus my sister there, complaining and dragging her feet. Besides, as we worked, my mother would tell stories about my grandmother and how she would clean house, or my mom would tell me stories about life during World War II. It was fun, really. The time flew by. You washed all of the curtains and ironed them. You flipped the mattresses and ironed the sheets and pillowcases. That's a "kick" of mine even now. I love resting my face upon an ironed and starched pillowcase. You scrubbed tub, sink and toilet and you used kerosene (Yes. Not a lot) to wipe down the ceramic tiles to make them shine like a mirror, and the pipes had better shine when you were done. And when she became a nurse, my mother taught us how to make a "hospital bed" with the proper corners. Served me well when I went into the army. At least at that, I was a step ahead of the rest. They even bounced a quarter on my bed one day in front of everyone. And that latrine sparkled. I only had bathroom duty once in basic training. That was all they needed to see I didn't see it as a form of punishment. I knew how to clean a bathroom. I used to clean my own house in Massachusetts the same damn way, all 13 rooms. By myself. No wonder I ended up needing two back surgeries. But even now, I wouldn't trade a moment of that time that I spent with my mom, cleaning those houses. I learned a lot about her, about her life, and about life in general. All it cost was a little sweat. I wonder some times how different life would have been if she had taken that time we had together to tell me the truth about my life.

And yet, I brought home great report cards. I was the only one in my family who actually enjoyed school. Heck, I was the only one of my immediate family to finish high school, granted it was a GED. Through it all though, I still made honor roll, was in the chorus, was in the band, and had the lead in my high school senior play. I buried everything that was going on at home, inside. I wasn't allowed to graduate because I flunked gym...I know. How stupid. But, the doctor gave me an excuse because my back problems had started even then. He presumed it was chronic and muscular in nature, and told me I was not to take gym, too strenuous. I took the excuse into school. My teacher refused to accept it. So, I was forced to decide. I chose to go by the doctor's ruling, and refused to take gym. They booted me out my senior year.

I also have to tell you that growing up I was a very quiet and shy kid. The perfect victim for abuse. I burrowed down even deeper into my self and stayed there, where I felt it was safest for me. I would have to say that I first noticed a change within myself when a friend introduced me to prescription diet pills...speed it was called. The street name at the time was robin's eggs because the pills were a speckled pale blue, like a robin's egg. The doctor is still in business back home. That one pill brought my personality, and more, right to the surface. I suddenly began to talk. And, my relatives couldn't believe what they were hearing. I remember vividly an uncle of mine asking one day, "What is the matter with you? You're so different, J." Oh, I was different, all right. I finally found my tongue and what I had to say was as bitter as battery acid. I finally started telling my family what I thought of them. I couldn't believe the difference in myself. Plus the fact that I trimmed down to nothing. After being called "Fatso" and "Queer" all my youth by my sisters and kids at school, there I was in my senior year of high school: tall, trim, fit, and not taking anybody's bullshit anymore. I had changed so much that I auditioned for the senior play that year and got one of the leads. Me, who didn't say "Shit," even if I had a mouth full. Oh, yea. These pills were G-R-REAT. I made the honor roll; I got a part in the play. I was finally doing it all. The only problem was that my friend forgot to tell me what it was like when you stopped taking the pills. Depression like you would not believe. I tried committing suicide at one point. Didn't take. My mother found me and having a psychiatric nurse as a mother did not help. She walked me for hours; back and forth, back and forth, pouring milk down my throat, and coffee. I was to tell no one about this episode. How could I do this to her? To her? I wasn't actually thinking of her when I downed the damn pills. I was thinking about my being gay, living in a hellhole like NEPA, in a family that was totally dysfunctional, and not having any way out that I could see for myself. Do it to her?? I learned a lot about my mother's view on life that long night we spent together. And, it was all about her.

I have never kidded myself about my mother. I worshiped her, but I knew her in a way my sisters never saw. When my father deserted us, I became more than her son; I became her friend, her business manager. I had to. There was no one else to help her. I raised my youngest sister while my mother worked. She had no other choice but to trust that I would be able to do it because she had to work. So, without ever questioning it, I did it. As I've said, when it's your everyday life, it becomes the norm. I raised my sister, I took care of the house, I collected my mother's paycheck and told her which bills had to be paid, I dealt with the bill collectors who couldn't be paid that month, I cooked the meals, cleaned the house, I did the laundry, I ironed her uniforms every day for work, and I even did her yearly taxes for her. I knew everything that came in and went out of that house. I was 14 years old, ladies and gentlemen. My mother didn't have the time for any of it, and didn't want to do it. After my father left, she wanted to avoid life. Actually, when my father left, my mother completely changed her life; not in a good way, either. She worked second shift and the year he left, she went out on New Year's Eve with some friends and that was probably the last we saw of her on a continual basis for about five years. She basically only came home to change her clothes. She went out every night after work with her friends.

At first, we were happy for her, because she had been so depressed after my father left and had lost so much weight, we were afraid something was going to happen to her, either mentally or physically. Maybe it should have. A breakdown would have been better than what she did do. She isolated herself from us. And, she never wanted to hear about our problems. It was sink or swim, and once again my instincts for surviving kicked in and I switched gears, took over running the house and raising my sister. That all came to a crashing halt about four years later, when my mother thought that I was being too strict with my sister. Okay, you take over, 'cause I'm damn tired of being a teenager and raising your kid. So, my mother took over raising my sister. What a disaster. My sister was out of school more than in, found a drug dealer for a boyfriend, and ended up on the banks of the Susquehanna River one night strung out from an overdose of pills while drinking wine with her friends. Okay, so thankfully one of them had enough sense to call the police and tell them where they could find her. She's rushed to the hospital but they can't treat her because she's under age. I come home from work to find a police officer sitting in our driveway, wanting to know where my mother is. Damn good question officer. She'd gone away for the weekend with one of her boyfriends and nobody knew where she was. So, I tracked down my oldest sister, we all went to the hospital, and they were able to treat my sister. A problem...my sister wouldn't tell anyone what happened or who was involved. I went into the treatment room and I talked with her. She told me everything. I turned around and told the police what they needed to know. Sorry, but they hurt my sister, someone I raised and had no problems with until my mother took over. And, at that point, I wanted my mother's blood. No one could find her. We had to wait until she blew into town to tell her what had happened. I stared at her when she walked in because I knew if I opened my mouth, I would have slapped her right across the face. I can understand mourning someone and I can understand feeling sorry for yourself. I cannot understand giving up on your family because someone has left you, and that someone was abusing your children. I saw my mother in an entirely different light that day, and she knew it and stayed away from me. One day about a week later, we were in the kitchen and I was not in the best mood, as things were still simmering inside about the nightmare we went through with my sister. For some reason, my mother told me to do something, as if

I was a kid again. I was washing dishes and without turning around, I said, "No, I'm not doing that." The next thing I knew, the large sauce pot was flying through the air, aimed at me. It bounced off of the wall and landed on the floor. I looked at my mother and she said, "I'm still your mother and you will do as I say." With that, MY Italian kicked in, and I picked up the pot from the floor and threw it right back at her, and I said, "I am sick of your shit. I don't feel one bit sorry for you, Mom. If this is how you want to live your life, go right ahead, but I am sick and tired of being the one who has to clean up the mess. And don't you ever do that again, or next time, I promise I won't miss." That was the day I became a young man. My mother and I reached a sort of truce. My older sisters chose to marry and run away. They've admitted as much to me over the years. Marriage was the only way they saw of getting out from under my mother's hand. I was gay. Marriage was out of the question. We were too poor for me to go to college. I couldn't have left at that point because she really did need my help. I learned that with my mother, you had to tear yourself away from her, bit by bit, because otherwise she would never let go of you. It was that day that I also realized I had to get out of there, I had to find a way to get away from her, or she'd continue to smother me as she had my entire life, never allowing my opinion, never being able to develop my own personality. It took years, but I did do it. I remember once telling my aunt, my mother's youngest sister, that my life would begin when my mother's ended. Thanks to Jackson, that's exactly what happened.

Chapter Six

"Fascination"
F.D. Marchetti and Franz Waxman
(My Parent's Song)

I used to visit my aunt, my father's sister. I liked her. My mother hated her. For years I stayed away from my father's family because of my mother's opinion of them. They had nothing to do with his leaving her, but I believe that since she couldn't vent her pain and anger on him because he'd disappeared, she threw it onto his family because they refused to tell her where he was. Anyway, I loved my aunt and my cousin, her daughter. One day, she called, and asked if I could come over for a visit. I went. My father was there. I hadn't seen him in probably ten years. In those years, I often wondered what I would do if I saw him again. I wasn't angry, I didn't want to punish him or hurt him. I wanted to hug him, and I did. I told him how much I missed him, how good it was to see him again. I know what you're thinking; he abused me. I caught him having sex with my cousin, the guy who had raped me. Yes, that's all true. But you forget that he was still my father. He was still the man who tucked me in at night when I was a kid, he was still the man who used to hold me in his lap and rub his stubbly beard on my neck and face because it tickled and made me laugh, he was still the man who carried me around on his shoulders through the house when my mother left her first husband, because he finally had his son with him. That was the man I chose to remember that day at my aunt's house. Now, it also happened that my mother's birthday was coming up in two days.

Every damn year my mother would say that the only thing she wanted was to see my dad again. That was all she ever asked for. That's right. I did it. I asked him if he would please come and see her, that she didn't hate him; none of us did. For whatever reason, he believed me. Before we left, I asked my father if I had been the reason he had left. He told me absolutely not, that his leaving had nothing to do with me. You see, for years my mother had blamed me for his leaving, because my father and I weren't getting along when he left. Anyway, he came with me. Off we went to my mother's house. I asked him to wait out on the back porch while I went in. My mother was in the living room and I sat beside her and told her that I had a surprise for her as a birthday present. She gave me one of her looks and said, "What ARE you up to son?" She only called me son when she was serious, so I told her to relax that I wanted to give her a birthday present now. I opened the back door, brought in my father and had him sit at the kitchen table like he always did before he left, and brought her into the kitchen. I don't think I've ever experienced a more emotional moment in my life. My mother stood there and you would have thought it was Christmas morning and I'd given her a mink coat. The smile on her face. The life that came back into her eyes. She put her hands to her face, and the tears came, as she stood there shaking her head back and forth. "Happy Birthday, Mom." I felt that I was intruding upon something special and so I left the two of them alone in the kitchen. The last thing I heard walking out into the back yard was my father saying, "Hi, hon. How've you been?" I stood out in the back yard, smoking a cigarette and the tears from all of those empty years exploded and came right to the surface before I even knew what had hit me. We had been a family, until something terrible split us up. We were one screwed-up mess of a family, but we were a family. I was never quite sure what it was that caused us to fall apart as a family but I knew that day that what we had been would never be again, even though I saw in that kitchen two people who still loved one another; more than they loved their children, even more than they loved themselves. After about 15 minutes, I went back in and they were still sitting there, talking. I told my father that maybe we should head back and he did the strangest thing; he asked my mother if he could walk through the house. She told him that he could. After he went upstairs, we looked at one another and she said to me, "Only you, only you could make my dream come true." I hugged her and told her that nothing was impossible, but she had better be careful next time for what she asked, and we both finally laughed. My father came downstairs and I guess he saw the looks on our faces of wondering what he was doing, and still being the shy man that I remembered, he had his hands in his pockets and put his head down and chuckled. Finally, he said to my mother, "I knew that you'd take care of them. I knew that they would be safe with you. I knew that you'd make it without me, and you have." As he walked out, my mother said, "Don't I even get a kiss goodbye this time?" It was the only time I ever saw my father cry. He looked at her and walked over to her and kissed her and held her in his arms for the last time. To me, my parents were like two halves of the same heart. They couldn't make it without each other, and didn't. Whatever mistakes they made, however they chose to live their lives away from one another, they were lost without each other. They both existed, just marked time. My parents never divorced.

Many years later, after my mother came to live with us, we talked about that surprise visit, and my mother told me what she talked about that day in the kitchen with my father. During the intervening years, my mother found out about my father's bisexuality and asked his sister if that information was true. His sister told her that it was, that my father had been like that for as long as they could remember, but no one had the heart to tell my mother. When my father visited that day, he asked my mother about coming back to live with us. When he did, she asked him about his bisexuality and he told her that it was true. She told him that she could have forgiven anything but that, because she knew that it was going on while they were together and that he had kept it from her, and her pride wouldn't allow her to take him back. How could she trust him ever again? That was the conversation I missed while I was in the back yard. That was why my father cried that day in the kitchen. My mother said, "No." Yet, she still wanted to kiss him and feel him in her arms one more time. What a mess. Why do we do these things to ourselves? Here were two people, crazy about each other still after being apart for over 12 years. One couldn't live without the other. God gave them the chance to come back together, and still my mother's pride wouldn't let her take the chance. She chose to be alone and unhappy for the rest of her life. The day she told me that story, I sat there, stunned. "But mom, you could have been happy. You could have had him back. That's what you always wanted, wasn't it?" "Oh no, I couldn't take him back, not once I knew the truth." The truth does not always set you free. Sorry, MLK, but what good did knowing the truth do for my mother? It kept her a prisoner within her own pain and heartache. And you know what; maybe I have lived my life to repeat my parent's mistakes in my relationships so that I could make a different choice. I always took Jackson back and maybe that's why. I don't know that for sure, but it wouldn't at all surprise me. We are our history.

Chapter Seven

"The Sins of the Father"

My father was born in White Stone, NY. His mother came from Ireland. His father I know nothing about.

I know very little of my father's background. My father was a very quiet man. Most of my memories of him come from my childhood. He left us when I was 14 and came back into my life very briefly during my twenties. That was the last I heard about, or from, my father until in my forties I was told of his death. Whether or not he was there physically, my father has been a part of my life every day, even now, 13 years after his death. And, in the Bible, where it says, "The sins of the father shall be paid for by the son," isn't that a hard nugget of truth.

My father was not the kindest person I've known, but as I grow older and look at our relationship, I realize that he had his own demons and they seemed to overtake him. I don't blame him for his behavior or hold him responsible for how he treated me. He was my father and I loved him, still do. Underneath it all, my father was a gentle, albeit tormented, soul.

My reason for writing about my dad now is that I went through some folders yesterday, looking for what I can't remember, and re-discovered some papers that I had received from my aunt after his death. Talk about opening a new chapter.

There, among old insurance policies and a copy of his death certificate, were his army discharge papers.

My father never discussed his life in the military, never. I was amazed by what I saw. My father enlisted in April 1941, before the attack on Pearl Harbor, right after his birthday. He was a photographer. I have no memory of my dad ever taking a picture. But he took and passed a photography course. Before his army days in Hawaii and the Philippines, dad served in the CCC camps in Quemado, New Mexico, in 1940. News to me. My father fought in the New Guinea campaign, the Philippine Islands campaign, and the attack on Pearl Harbor. He received three bronze battle stars, the Asiatic Pacific Theater ribbon, the Philippine Liberation ribbon, and the American Defense Service ribbon with Bronze Star. All of this from this tall, lanky, quiet man who preferred working the N.Y. Times' Sunday crossword amongst his encyclopedia set and dictionaries spread over his bedroom floor, and would become my father when he turned 38. Whew. A totally different person from the one I knew as "dad."

When I think of dad, I think of Christmas. I've never seen anything like it. He just loved Christmas. He made the holiday for us when we were kids. People think that I get my personality from my mother. In part, I have her sense of duty to responsibility, and her loyalty to friends, wanting to help others, sense of family ties, etc., but my joy for life and in living comes from my father. Fifty years later, I realize what an amazing man he really was. His war record thrills me. How I wish I could talk with him about it and his experiences. My father's life was much like my own. How sad that he lived long enough to see his history repeated but not long enough to see that I survived it and healed, and still love him.

My paternal grandmother emigrated from Ireland, taking a job as a domestic. She became pregnant via Mr. Barnes and gave birth to my father. How they ended up in NEPA, minus Mr. Barnes, is still a mystery to me. I was told that she met a Mr. S. in NEPA, never married, and had three more children; M, J & C. She and her brood settled in as a unit, Mr. S. exiting the picture as well. However, my father took the surname of his stepfather. I know very little about his family except for the time we spent with them when I was a child. Until I was about seven, we were very close with my dad's family.

When my mother left her first husband, five years after my birth, we moved in with my aunt and her two children, in this huge, old Victorian house. My love for architecture began right there. That house was a kid's delight. It had servant's quarters on the third floor, which was where we played, a servant's back stairway, a wonderful wrap-around porch, and a huge, gorgeous main stairway with a landing at a beautiful stained-glass window. And, that is where I spent three wonderful years of my childhood, where I went halloweening, and where I spent Christmases as a young child. My first experience with someone dying, with someone's birth, the place where I buried my first pet, my turtle "Sam"; all the moments spent creating and living a young life, along with living through some traumas, were spent there.

My love of animals comes from my dad. My mom hated pets. They dirtied her house. She took more kittens and puppies that I dragged home for a "ride," no wonder I have abandonment issues and cling to people I love. On any given day, you could walk into my parent's bedroom and open a drawer and find a bird wearing a splint, or a squirrel with a chewed tail that was wrapped and healing. You had no idea what dad had dragged in. It used to drive my mom crazy. But, what a wonderful experience for me as a kid. When I think back, I wonder what my parents saw in each other. They were so different. Maybe that was the attraction.

Living in that wonderful house, I was able to experience the luxury of discovering things. Sitting here, 45 years later, I can still remember playing in that attic, of how it smelled when you opened the attic door in the summer and that wave of heat would hit you as you climbed the attic steps. That memory still exists for me as strong as the day it was created. My happiest moments as a child were spent in that house.

The first trauma I can remember experiencing was the death of my cousin, B. My cousin was a year or two older than me. We used to play together in that house. I don't remember the event itself, but it impacted upon my life for years afterward as I was the last to see him alive.

What I recall is one very hot summer day. My mother was watching the two of us, as my aunt was away. We were outside playing in our yard, wandering over to a neighbor's driveway where a car engine was sitting in parts on the concrete. Somewhere, B. found matches and as we sat there, he kept striking the matches and throwing them at the engine's pieces. Suddenly, I heard my mother calling for us to come in for our naps. I got up and went in, leaving B. there. That is all I recall of that hot, lazy summer day. The rest is blocked out.

My mother had called for B. when she put me down for my nap, but he didn't come in. She said that she went back to the kitchen and called out to him, when she heard him start screaming. She ran out to the side yard but didn't see him, and she looked over the incline in our back yard toward our neighbor's house, toward the direction of the screams and saw the fire. As she ran toward our neighbor's driveway, she had the forethought to grab towels from our clothesline, thinking she'd need them. She remembered that as she came to the top of the incline, B. had stopped screaming. When she got to the driveway, she couldn't find B. Apparently, one of the matches had hit the engine and the gasoline had ignited. B. was close enough that it engulfed him in flames. She couldn't recognize him because being summer, he wasn't wearing much clothing and his skin was exposed to the flames, so he was charred, along with the engine parts. Then, he moved and moaned. She said that was when she found him and threw the towels on him to protect him from what was left of the fire. When she got to him and tried to move him, he began screaming again. So, she ran back to the house and called the fire department and called my father to come home. My little cousin lived for several hours after they got him to the hospital. He was severely burned over most of his body. Only his groin area and his feet were not charred because his clothing covered them. As my aunt was away, the decisions to be made for B's treatment were left up to my father. So, there stood my mother and father, two quiet unassuming people, caught up in the midst of this terrible nightmare. And, as my mother would tell me many years later, I slept through it all, not knowing anything of what had happened.

My aunt wanted B. laid out at home. What she couldn't have realized at the time was that the undertaker had to literally rebuild B. out of wax from a portrait that had been painted of B. and his sister: arms, legs, head and face, all a wax representation. The problem? It was summer. B. was laid out at home. B. began to melt. B. was buried.

The other tragedy brought on by B's death was that my father could not forgive his sister for having gone away. You see, she was having an affair with a married man, even though she herself was married at the time to an Army career man. No one could find her to tell her what had happened and everything fell onto my parents. And, that was what led to our moving out of that wonderful house.

For years after that, well into my twenties, I had an unknown fear of matches. I had no idea what had happened to B. The subject was never discussed. I wasn't even there for the funeral. I was shipped off to another aunt's house, away from it all. My aunt kept the portrait of B. & E. in her living room, but she rarely talked about him and you didn't ask. She kept her loss and her memories to herself.

B's death however caused my parents to be even more protective of me. I never left their sight and was always within arm's reach of my mother.

As I grew much older, my mother told me what had happened to B. because there were times when my aunt would call and ask my mother if I could go and visit with her. She was always very kind to me and wanted me there to mother me, I think. We would talk about school, what I wanted to do when I grew up, etc. I kept her company and we never talked about B.

And, that was my first experience with death and loss. A year later, my cousin J. drowned. Believe me, my every move was monitored. My parents were not about to lose me. How to do this? By not allowing me to do anything; no sports, no bike, no paper route, no wandering off with friends - nothing - and no swimming. I was allowed one diversion - books. Reading was harmless. Reading was allowed. At about ten, I was finally allowed a bike. An old rust bucket with no metal trim and bare tires, but it was mine. My first taste of freedom. I still get the same thrill of escaping when I get into my car - where am I going, what will I discover, who will I meet? It's still there. I still do most of my thinking and decision making while I'm driving.

Chapter Eight

"Penn's Woods..."

Pennsylvania. What can I say? It translates to "Penn's woods." I grew up in NEPA and it always left me with a feeling of wanting; for what, I was never quite sure, but I knew it wasn't to be found there. I am usually very critical in my opinion of my home town, but that is only because I always sensed what it could have been. It had a great start, like many other towns during the early period of the industrial revolution that exploded overnight into major cities of that era. Its location was perfect for expansion. It lies between and southwest of New York City and due north of Philadelphia. All trains led to NEPA. It had industry; steel plants, silk mills, major train yards for connecting with points north, south and west. It had clothing manufacturing, coal mines, iron furnaces for the production of steel, and lace mills. A center of higher education. And, lest we forget, it was once the King of Coal. It also had a cheap and plentiful labor force, still does. Unfortunately, it also had/has a well-oiled political machine, which wanted a cut of everything. Ask anyone of my mother's generation about NEPA during World War II and they will tell you that it was famous for its whorehouses. Yep, a little enclave of "cat houses" that were nestled in on the other side of the train station and tracks, just outside of town. How convenient.

Talk about one-stop shopping. And even in that "industry," the politicians made sure they got their cut. That stubborn, greedy point of view is what has led to the demise of northeastern Pennsylvania. Going there, you seem to enter a time warp as you drive through the mountains and enter Lackawanna Valley. I have talked to many people who have gone there, either to live or visit, and they basically have all said the same thing. A totally different breed of human exists there. Very nice people, usually friendly and helpful, but while you're talking with them there is a sense of something not being quite right and you begin to wonder if maybe the water has been tampered with and it would be better not to drink from it and get out while you can. It's a very odd and unsettling feeling, but anyone with more than two brain cells will tell you that there is an undercurrent of disquiet that you feel while you're there that makes you want to leave and get back to the real world. There is a mist of ignorance that hangs unnoticed over that area which nothing seems able to dispel.

My childhood and early years weren't a total hellish experience, it just seemed that way mainly because of living in such a depressing place as NEPA. It was and is a pit of oppression and suppression of the people there; no sense of self-worth or human value is instilled into the population, no sense of pride in their history or ancestors. Political corruption is the mainstay and always has been. You think that the old political machines are dead in this country? A thing of the past? Go spend some time in NEPA. Political favoritism abounds in NEPA. Gay politicians, plenty. Even some gay judges. Of course, all married and playing the "game" to get what they want. Murder? Enough to make your blood run cold; some rather infamous cases, too, involving some very wealthy and well-known citizens of local, state, national AND international fame and public service.

There is a murder mystery from the 1930's that has always fascinated me. It's still listed as an unsolved murder, but anyone who remembers it will tell you they knew all along who murdered the poor girl. She had gone out on a job interview and was never again seen alive. She had been tortured before finally being killed, in a shed out in the woods. It was said that people living in the hills at the time could hear her screams during the night as she was being tortured, but they had no idea who it was. The only way they found her body was that in searching the woods they came upon a creek, frozen over in spots due to the harsh winter weather, and one man spotted a hand sticking up out of the water, as if signaling them for help to find her.

There is another case of a young student who was walking home from school and was enticed into getting into a car with two adults. The driver was male; the other passenger was stated as looking like a man, but dressed as a woman. The boy's body was later found in the woods. He had been raped and sodomized. The initial news reports talked about two adults in the car. Suddenly, the story switched to involving one adult. How he was able to drive the car and entice the boy to get in has never been disclosed. Who the second passenger was remains an unanswered question. Many years later I worked in a mental hospital. There was a nurse I worked with there and we got around to talking about this story one night. She told me that she remembered the case well, because at the time she had been a nurse in the emergency room of a hospital back home, a hospital where the boy's body was brought when it was found. The police officers were discussing the case in front of her. They knew there were two adult men involved; however, one of the men, the one dressed to look like a woman, was the son of a very prominent state official, a favorite son of NEPA. Thus, the story went out that it involved only one male adult. All covered up with everyone promptly paid off, including some officials involved "retiring" and moving away. Even the hospital is now gone; torn down. The one adult male found was discovered to have been a former mental patient, who had killed before. He was placed into a high-security facility for the criminally insane. Locked up in one of the back wards to live out the rest of his tortured days away from society and away from being questioned by anyone about the case, who was involved, or if he had actually done it alone.

There is the infamous case of a local physician who put five bullets into his wife, several of which went directly into her face from point-blank range, and he claimed that she was trying to commit suicide and he was trying to get the gun away from her. And, believe it or not, the poor soul lived until the paramedics arrived. They found her all wrapped up and buried under blankets and pillows on the bed. Can you imagine the agony? The alleged rumor to this day is that he got off and moved to another country, where he may still be practicing medicine. Any wonder why people flee that area as soon as they can.

Let's see, who is famous and from NEPA (Which means that they were smart enough to get the hell out while they could). Well, there is a film actress, a star in the 1940s and 1950s, who had her contract cancelled at a major film studio when they invoked the "morals" clause. The only time that has been known to happen in Hollywood; and, a child actress/singer at Universal in the 1940s and claimed NEPA as her home (I believe that she was born in Buffalo, NY, though). There is a writer who was married to a NY Times film critic, and of course more recently came a famous playwright/actor, now deceased. And, this is what I mean about the thick-headedness of NEPA's political machine. Here is this world-famous prize-winning playwright, as well as having been an actor who accomplished an international level of fame. The poor man died IN NEPA a few years back and I believe is buried there, and they're fighting over where a statue of this genius should be placed. As far as I know, it has yet to be placed anywhere. There were a pair of brothers, famous Hollywood screenwriters and one a director as well of some of the biggest Hollywood films of the 1940-1950 era. There is also a world-renowned urban planner recently deceased, who is from NEPA. No matter who I meet or where, when they hear where I'm from, they almost always say, "Oh, I've driven through there." Yea, and kept right on going...lucky you.

Chapter Nine

In the Arms of the Angels

One of the brightest lights in my life was my niece, Pam. Whenever I tell people that I believe there are angels among us, I'm speaking of my niece. She was that—an angel.

My niece was born mentally retarded and with cerebral palsy. In her early twenties, she was found dead in bed at Christmas. I was living in France at the time and had called home to wish my family a merry Christmas, but no one answered. No one answered at my sister's house. So I called my other sister's house. Again, no one answered. I kept trying and finally got through after Christmas. My sister told me what had happened.

Being so far away, I was always so concerned that something would happen to my mother. Instead, it was Pammie who died unexpectedly. Her heart stopped. She died in her sleep. Our beautiful little Pamela. We thought of her beauty as her curse. You see, as a child, she looked normal. Strangers would walk up to my sister and ask about her because she was so beautiful, and slowly it would register that there was something wrong with her—and they would walk away. She was the most beautiful baby and child. She had the most beautiful, almond-shaped eyes and the most lustrous hair I have ever seen. She did recognize voices, and when I would come in and yell, "Hello,

Pammie!" she would get so excited. She couldn't walk, and she couldn't talk, but God could she smile. And laugh. I used to love to get her laughing. In talking with my sister, I realized that I couldn't reach them because of the funeral, which I had missed. So, I told my sister that I would come home as soon as I could.

When I got off the phone, I totally lost it. Jackson and his daughter had gone out for dinner while I stayed home to keep trying to call my family. When they came home, I was sitting in the study in our apartment, all wrapped up in a blanket, crying quietly, remembering my beautiful niece. I told Jackson that I had to leave; I had to go home and see my sister to make sure she was going to be all right. I left from Paris the next day. It was a long flight. I don't remember most of it because I spent the time trying to think of something that I could tell my sister to prove to her that Pammie's life did have meaning, that her existence did matter.

And so, I spent the time reliving my niece's short life, and in doing that, I came to the realization that she was an angel. I came to finally understand that she had been a gift given to us, only we chose to see her as some tragically flawed being. The flaw was ours, not hers. We could have learned so much from her had we only opened our hearts while we had her with us. Instead, we chose to pity her.

My little niece endured things that would have driven me mad. From infancy, she had a set schedule every day. When she got up, we had to give her peanut butter and pray to God that she would choke on it to develop her gag reflex. She endured salt baths, where we mixed salt and enough water to make a paste and sat her in the sink and proceeded to rub this mixture all over her body until her skin was blood red. That was to stimulate her nerve endings. Her daily routine consisted of physical therapy, where my sister had to come up with a list of different people: a team of three, three times a day, every damn day of the week. That was to keep her limber, and it had to be different people in the hopes that she would develop a sense of touch and know the different touches of different hands. She had a sliding board with

Christmas lights attached to either side that she had to make her own way down looking at the lights as they flashed. You had to take her into a dark closet and sit there turning a small, lighted, colored bulb on and off for a period of minutes. I believe these two were to strengthen her vision, but I'm not sure any more. There was so much to do, and it had to be done every day. Not to mention the trips to Philadelphia for her checkups or the operations she endured. My sister kept a big bulletin board on her kitchen wall with the names of who was scheduled for the different days.

We lived next door, so if someone couldn't make it, over we would go. I was happy to be of help. I used to babysit for my sister quite often. Pam was adorable. I loved rocking her to sleep. We had to be very careful when holding her because she had a shunt that ran from the base of her skull to her chest, which, I believe, connected to her heart. The slightest jerk could dislodge it, which would cause her to suffer severe pressure on her brain from the fluid collecting. And yet, she could smile at you. An angel? Yes, indeed.

My niece lived in a world where she only knew love. She never knew anger or hatred, never experienced envy or deliberate cruelty for another, and never had a broken heart. She only knew love. That was what we missed during her life. That was what we never experienced—the knowledge that here in our laps sat the epitome of God's love and innocence. We were too blinded by the physical. In actuality, we were the cripples. We were crippled emotionally because we could not see beyond her physical presence what God had really given us. I only realized this after her death.

And when I arrived home, I sat down with my sister, and I saw the defeat in her eyes, the idea that all of those years had been wasted. I told her I had something to tell her, something that I didn't realize until it was too late, but that I wanted to share with her. I told her of my flight home. I hoped that it made a difference for her. It couldn't bring my niece back to us, but it gave her life validity. As I finished speaking, I saw that recognition in her eyes.

I will always, always love my niece. I will always thank God for having brought that little angel into my life. I will always be grateful to Him for letting me see how special she was and what her being in our lives meant, and I will always be proud to have known her. She was a light in my life, that little girl. She was an angel.

There were others, too.

I had what I consider to be two guardian angels in my life when I was growing up: my maternal grandfather and my uncle T, my mother's brother-in-law. My grandfather was the kindest, gentlest man I have ever known. I remember when I went to see *The Godfather.* When Marlon Brando opened his mouth to speak, I froze because he sounded just like my grandfather. I sat in the theatre and closed my eyes and went back in time, remembering that dear, sweet man.

My grandfather came to America from Italy with his father and his brother. His father eventually returned to Italy to bring the rest of his family to America. He never came back. And so, these two brothers made their own way in America; one settling in Pennsylvania, the other eventually working his way up to the Buffalo area. There is a cemetery where I come from where four generations of my family have worked, starting with my great-grandfather (my maternal grandmother's father), to my grandfather (his son-in-law) and my great-uncle Tony (my grandfather's brother-in-law), to my mother's first husband, and both of my first brother's-in-law (my older sister's first husbands). As I grew up, everyone looked at me as if it was my rite of passage, and I said, "You're kidding." There was NO way I was digging graves for a living. Not that I was ashamed of it, I couldn't stand being around dead people. It was so final. My ancestors laid the stone paths in that place. My grandfather and great-uncle built the grottos that still hold the statues in that cemetery. When we were children, my mother would take us to the cemetery regularly, and we would have picnics there, because it is located on a sweeping hillside in the valley that offers a panoramic view of the mountains and lower valley. Absolutely beautiful. My mom would tell us, "Never fear the dead. It's the living you have to be afraid of." So, we would go there and "visit" all of our relatives, pull the weeds and clean around their stones and markers. They became another extension of our family, and my mom would sit there and tell us stories about each of them, about their lives. We would sit with my great-uncle Tony, her uncle who worked there, and he would ask me about school and my grades, and tell me that I had to be good in school so I wouldn't end up digging graves for a living (See, I listened). He was a great guy, Uncle Tony. He was my grandmother's brother. Her other brother Mike was the one who killed himself. Her sister Angela died in childbirth, and she had a sister, Rose. Rose and Tony were the only two left. My grandmother had died of a stroke when she was 50. I think we went to the cemetery so often because my mother never got over her own mother's death. We would go to her grave and my mom would sit there and talk with her. I would take my sister and walk around the stones, showing her the different phrases that had been imbedded into the stone, so that my mother could have some time alone with her mother, and we would go and talk with my grandfather and Uncle Tony.

I trailed off here, somehow. My grandfather. One of my earliest memories is of going to see my grandfather at his house and he would take me by the hand and into the parlor we would go. He would sit down on the couch with me and ask how I was doing in school (Again, with the grades. But, I listened), and he would put his hand in mine and he would give me a quarter. Every time I saw him. That was our "meeting," and he would kiss me and we would go back and join the others. However, for years, I wasn't allowed in my grandfather's house. My Uncle J. had married and he and his wife had moved into my grandfather's house and basically never left. I can still remember their wedding. My grandfather walked me to the church from his house. God, I think I was no more than five or six at the time, in my suit strutting up the street to the church, holding my grandfather's hand. It was because of my "heritage" that I wasn't allowed into my grandfather's house. My mother never told me why, but we would go to the cemetery to visit my grandfather. Gosh, he was the smallest guy. This little Italian, so soft-spoken, but everyone listened to him. My mother always called him, "Pa." She never disrespected him and never smoked in front of him. He hated that she dyed her hair. My mother was a blonde for as long as I can remember. He hated it. I remember one day being in our car and my mother was talking with my grandfather at the cemetery, and he suddenly asked her, "Why you don't come to the house anymore to visit?" Now, that was the first time I remember my mother being stumped for something to say. This was her father and she didn't want to upset him, but he had her cornered. So, she told him. Her brother had told her that he didn't want her coming to the house with me. What struck me and is why I remember it so vividly, is that my mother couldn't look at her father when she told him. She kept her head down. I remember my grandfather pushing away from the car, standing there looking at us, and he said looking right at me, "That is my house, not your brother's. You be there Sunday at noon, with my grandson." My grandfather never yelled. I haven't a memory of him raising his voice to anyone, but when he spoke, they listened. We went on Sunday at noon. My uncle never said a word about our being there. My aunt served us and acted as if nothing was wrong, as if we came every Sunday, and my grandfather took me into the parlor and gave me a quarter, as he always did. That attitude lasted until he died. When he was taken to the hospital, my Uncle J. told my mother that he didn't want the grandchildren going to the hospital to see grandpa because it might scare him. No one had told him that he was dying, just that he was ill. So, I couldn't go and see him. I was allowed one visit at his house before he was taken to the hospital. My aunt was visiting from Detroit, to help take care of him. I wanted to see her, as she was my godmother, and so I went to my grandfather's house. I was allowed to go upstairs to see him because he heard me talking downstairs. So, they had to let me go up and see him. Of course, I was given strict instructions on what to say, not to stare at him, and to smile. So, up I went, all alone. It dawned on me as I climbed those stairs that I had never been in my grandfather's bedroom. What would I expect to find? So, in I went. There was my dear grandpa, so small in that bed, so sick. He had cancer and I remember this huge swelling on the side of his neck. He had a tumor that had wrapped itself around the carotid on the left side of his neck and they couldn't operate on him. That was a long time ago. So, it was slowly choking him to death, cutting off his air supply. He wanted to know how I was doing, how school (I was a junior in high school) was and my grades (Again with the grades). I told him that I was fine; school was fine...all the while I wanted to tell him how much I loved him and what he had meant to me as a grandfather, but I knew that I couldn't. I did do one thing though that I hadn't done in years. When I was leaving, I went over to him to hold his hand. It seemed so weak and small in mine, I remember. I leaned over and kissed his forehead, telling him that I loved him and hoped he would get better soon, and he smiled at me. As I left, he said in that Marlon Brando whisper of his, "Eh, my boy." I turned around and looked at him and he raised his arm and waved to me, and I knew that he knew he was dying. I walked slowly down those steps and into the kitchen, out into the back yard where my grandfather had built a low stone wall many years before. I sat out there and remembered being a kid and running to the back of the yard where he had a huge vegetable garden. He would give me a bag and tell me to go and get some "mangoes" for my mother (Mangoes where I come from are what Italians called peppers). I remembered the grape arbor he had; how sweet the grapes smelled in the summer and as a kid, sitting there under the arbor inhaling that sweet scent, knowing that they would be picked for grandpa's Dego Red wine. I sat there and remembered coming to the house when he made his homemade sausage and hung it on the enclosed back porch to dry and cure. I remembered because I knew that when he died, all of that would go with him, and it did. My grandfather went into the hospital shortly after that visit. He was dying. I remember being in school one day and having a friend of my aunt's who worked at the school, stopping me in the hall and offering her condolences to me upon my grandfather's death. I told her that I didn't know what she was talking about, that he was still alive. She told me that I should go home for the day. I was very confused because at that point, I didn't even know that he was in the hospital. So, I went home, but my mother wasn't there. Instead, friends of hers were there, and they told me that it was true. He had gone into the hospital and my mother was there and yes, he had died. That was how I found out that my dear grandfather was gone. I went out onto the back porch and sat on the steps and I don't think I have ever cried so much in my life. It caught me totally off guard. He was gone. Grandpa was gone. I sat there crying and remember my mother coming home and she stood there and stared at me, and not saying anything, she went into the house. I've never understood her reaction. I cried for hours. Family came by and I sat there, crying. My aunt and uncle came in from Buffalo and stayed with us and all I could do was cry. And then came the viewing. I only went to one, the one for the family.

My Uncle B. from Buffalo came with me. I'll never forget him for doing that. A wonderful man, whom I didn't know that well because they lived so far away. But, a great guy. An alcoholic, but a sweetheart of a guy. I used to love sitting there, listening to his stories while he drank. He drove my Aunt D. nuts, but I thought he was wonderful. A big, burly guy, who couldn't stand his wife's family, except for my mother and us. I think I loved him for that alone. He used to tell my mother's family exactly what he thought of them. "Those crazy Wops. They think their shit don't smell" was a favorite of his. Once, my mother's family went to visit my Aunt D. in Buffalo. A whole crop of them trekked there for a visit. Well, when my mother's family spoke, you listened. They were the clan, didn't you know? Yea, THAT breed of Italian, the embarrassing breed. They always sat together at weddings and funerals, never bothering with other people. Anyway, they drive to Buffalo and "appear" at my aunt's house, and my Uncle B. threw ALL of them out, except for my mother. She could stay. The odd thing is that my mother was the only one who ever told my Uncle B. what a crock he was and that her sister was crazy for marrying him. But, he loved my mother. Probably because she was the only one who told him to his face what she thought of him. But, we were always welcome in their house and they were always welcome in our house. There's a story my mother used to tell me about my Uncle B. and Aunt D. It was early in their marriage and they had been arguing. Well, my Aunt D. calls my mother and tells her to come to the house that B. had been drinking and had a shotgun. Well, we only lived a couple of blocks from them at the time and over she treks, with her brother, my godfather. So, they're skulking in the bushes in my aunt's back yard and they can hear them arguing. Out onto the porch comes Aunt D. My mother runs up to her, and she hands my mother the baby. She runs back into the house and argues some more with my Uncle B. She runs out onto the porch again, this time with my her oldest child, who was probably three years old. My mother grabs him. What does my Aunt D. do? She runs BACK into the house and argues some more with my Uncle B. There's my mother and my uncle holding the two kids, in the bushes, waiting for my Aunt D. and she's in the house still arguing with my Uncle B. The next thing they see is my Aunt D. come running out the back door and down the path, not stopping for any of them yelling, "Jesus, he loaded the gun. Run!!!!" And there comes my Uncle B., loaded shotgun and all onto the back porch, aiming it at my Aunt D. and pulls the trigger. **BOOM**... There's my mother and my uncle, stuck in the bushes in between my uncle with the gun, and there's my Aunt D., running down the street, screaming. No idea where my mother is with her kids, she's just running to get away from my uncle. Mind you, this was in the 1950's, and it was thought of as a "domestic problem." He told the cops he was trying out the rifle for hunting season. And, that's life in NEPA, ladies and gentlemen. You would have to have heard my mother tell that story. She would have us roaring.

My aunt never forgot it, either. At that point, my uncle came to western New York looking for work, my aunt chased after him, and my mother raised my cousins for over a year. That's being Italian. When my mother and her sisters and brothers would get together and start talking about growing up and living during World War II, you would sit there and roar until you cried.

Anyway, my Uncle B. comes with me to the funeral home. God, I dreaded walking into that place, knowing I'd have to see my grandfather in his coffin. I must tell you that I had dreamt of his dying for about a week before it actually happened. It was the same dream, over and over; I was walking up a hill and at the top stood a house with a white-picket fence, and behind the fence at the gate sat my grandfather, smiling at me and waiting for me to get to the top of the hill, where he sat. As I did, he reached out and touched my face. End of dream. I always woke up at that point. I told my mother about my dreams, that something was going to happen, but still I couldn't accept that he had actually died. I used to freak my mother out with my dreams. I don't know how or why they started, they just did, when I was a teenager. My suspicion would be that my being raped and my withdrawing even more into myself is what set them off. I don't know for sure. So, we went into the funeral home. There are two scents that I absolutely hate and that make me immediately sick to my stomach; one is the smell of alcohol in a doctor's office. I always associate it with getting a needle and I hate needles, so therefore I hate the smell of alcohol in a doctor's office. The other is the smell of flower arrangements in a funeral home. God, isn't that scent overpowering when you first walk into a funeral home? I can't stand it. Whenever I walk into a funeral home, which is almost never, I stand there and take a deep breath to absorb the shock of that scent. We walked over to his coffin and there he was. Grandpa. And, he looked so sad. He actually had a frown upon his face. Everyone noticed it. Poor grandpa. They had lied to him, even at the end. Now they had to deal with his look of disappointment in his children for lying to him. I knew it as soon as I looked at his face. What I remember most about his funeral is that after everyone left the cemetery and had gone back to his house, my mother wanted me to walk with her back to the cemetery to be alone with him. The cemetery was only two or three blocks from where my grandfather had lived. I wasn't crazy about the idea but I knew that if I didn't she would have gone on her own, so I went with her. We got there as they were about to load the dirt in on top of his coffin. I will never do that again. It was my mother's family that was finishing the burial, in respect for my grandfather; my great-uncle Tony, my brother's-in-law were there and my mother's first husband. They were all there, waiting, not knowing what to do with my mother standing there. I looked at them and nodded my head to begin the process. I felt that she needed to see it to understand that he was really gone. I stood there and held her while she cried for her father. It isn't one of my happiest memories, but it's a memory that I carry. It now strikes me how I happened to be there for a lot of the significant moments in my mother's later life. I never realized that before now. I wonder what that means.

Shortly after his death, my mother's family all agreed to sign over my grandfather's house to her brother and sister-in-law, since they were living there and had taken care of my grandfather while he was ill. I don't think it was quite six months later and they had gutted the entire house, torn out the gardens and grape arbor. Gone, everything was gone. I went back to that house maybe two or three times, but couldn't stand being there, it was that different. Plus the fact that my uncle's word was law and we weren't exactly welcome. But, I had my say before leaving for good. My Aunt M., my godmother, had divorced her husband and moved to Detroit. My Aunt D. came in for a visit and was staying with us, and she and my mother were talking about M's "move." It turned out that my Aunt M. moved to Detroit to live with an old flame of hers. They had dated years and years before, but my grandmother wouldn't allow her to marry him because he wasn't Catholic. Now, they were living together because he was getting a divorce. Living together? Yes, living together. The exact same "sin" for which my mother had been tormented for years by her family, and for which I paid a price because I was the product of her relationship with my father. Hmm...This didn't add up in my book. Why was it all right for Aunt M. to do, but a sin for my mom to have committed? That did it. Without telling anyone, I drove to my uncle's house and knocked on the door. It was a Sunday afternoon and I stood there, remembering the many Sundays that I wasn't allowed into that house to see my grandfather. My uncle opened the door and stood looking, not letting me enter. I proceeded to tell him what I thought of him, his wife, his family AND especially his sister M., and what they could do with their stupid opinions. I told him how he had made me feel when I was growing up, how I hated him for not letting me see my grandfather, how I thought for years that he was actually gay and covering it with his stupid marriage to what appeared to me to be a Polish lesbian; I just let him have it all, and I told him they could ALL go to hell, and I walked away. He never uttered a word...he couldn't. You see, he hadn't put in his false teeth before opening the front door. Well, I no sooner got home and there was my mother in the kitchen, waiting for me. "Your Uncle J. called me." "Yea?" "Yes, and he told me all about your conversation at the front door." I stood there, waiting for her usual lecture about how I needed to respect my elders, that this was my uncle AND my godfather, blah, blah, blah. Nothing like that at all. She looked at me and said, "It's about damn time someone told my family what hypocrites they really are. I never had the guts because they're my family. I couldn't do it while your grandfather was alive, and I didn't care after he died. Thank you for loving me so much, son." No matter what has happened before or since; no matter what I have discovered or surmised about my mother's behavior toward me, I still love her every bit as much.

The other angel in my life was my Uncle T. What a gem. He was your typical Irishman; red hair and temper to match, but a great sense of humor. I swear I learned to laugh at life from watching how my Uncle T. dealt with his. There will never be another like him, I swear, and how very much I still miss him every day. A wonderful man. He was more of a father to me when I needed one than anyone else. He kept an eye out for me and on me, to make sure I walked the straight and narrow. But, I was crazy about him. Another family story. From the stories my mother told me, my Aunt A. was quite the party girl during World War II. She had her share of "callers" in her youth. God only knows how many guys she was engaged to at the same time, but that was her business. I only tell these stories about my mother's family because these were the same people who judged her when she lived openly with my father, unmarried, and passed that same judgment onto me. Hypocrites. Anyway, my Aunt A. tangled with the wrong one when she met T. Before you knew it, his parents were at my grandparent's house to discuss marriage, as my aunt was...preggers, as the English say. My mother always claimed that my grandmother never got over the shock of that, which led to her first stroke. She was too ashamed to leave her house after that happened. The irony of it all is that my cousin was born on my grandmother's birthday. Sort of God's way of never letting my aunt forget her indiscretion. But, back to my Uncle T. I adored him. You know, the more I think of it, I realize that I adored ALL of my aunt's husbands in my mother's family, because they didn't take any of my relative's nonsense. They told them exactly what they thought of them, and why. When I would go to my Aunt A's house (They lived a block away from us), it was usually when I knew my Uncle T. was home. He'd always be perched in his Laz-Y-Boy with his cigarettes and his beer. That was his routine. He had a pet name for me that he always called me when he saw me. Didn't matter where he saw me; I could be walking home from school and he'd be on his front porch, or I'd walk into his house and there he'd be in his recliner. No one else ever called me that name. I still cherish that nickname because he gave it to me, and I haven't allowed anyone else ever to use it when they address me. That was something between Uncle T. and me. My ex- tried calling me that and the first time he did it, I told him, "Don't even go there. You don't know me well enough to call me by that name." I explained to him what that name meant to me. He never called me that again. To me, that was special turf. No one went there. Oddly, it was my Uncle T's son who raped me. I think he envied the relationship I had with his father, one he didn't share. They were NOT close. Again, oddly enough, he was close with my father, which I'm sure helped ease the pain of awkwardness when I caught them in bed together. Very Freudian, wouldn't you say? I wonder if my cousin planned all of that the way it happened to get even with me. I don't know. But, I'm sure that was one of the reasons for his raping me: power and intimidation. Rape is all about domination. I had something he would never have. His father loved me as I was. I have to admit that in writing this story, I begin to see the routine of daily chaos in which I grew up and lived. No wonder everything now should seem so anticlimactic. Not a day went by that there wasn't some sort of emergency. The days I spent running to relative's houses to hide from my father, or to get help because he was drunk and beating up my mother. It was unending. It also gave me a rather skewed view of what a relationship really is. But, back to my Uncle T.

There is no point in defending my uncle's alcoholism. He was an alcoholic. As long as I knew him, my uncle drank. He worked for the railroad and I don't know how many times co-workers had to drag him off the tracks because he had either passed out or fallen asleep. Personally, I think that my uncle was suicidal and those episodes were planned. As I grew older, probably starting at 11 or 12 years of age, my Aunt A. would call and ask my mother if I could come down and sit with my uncle. It usually happened when he was drunk and my aunt and my cousins would scatter, trying to avoid him and is behavior. So, I would trek to my aunt's house and she'd leave me with him. When he had been drinking, he always called my mother, threatening to jump off the bridge. Where I come from, there was a bridge that was a popular "jumping-off" point for people. She would listen, joke with him, and get him to talk about something else, or wait until he fell asleep while talking. Usually, if she knew he was alone, she'd tell me to go to my aunt's house and keep an eye on him until someone there came home. It amazes me to think that they'd ask a kid to keep watch. What would I have done if something happened? I guess they figured that if I was there, he wouldn't do anything. Still, that's taking a BIG chance. But, I'd go. I loved him and loved being with him. He never questioned what I was doing there or tried putting me out. I was welcome. And, the stories would begin. My uncle had served in the Pacific during World War II. He'd been put in the blockade for decking his sergeant one night. I told you, a crazy Irishman, my Uncle T. Two evenings involving my Uncle T. I still carry with me. One night, we were in his bedroom, and he told me to go to the closet and bring out his scrapbooks. So, I did. As I sat down on the bed, I opened them and there was his life spread out before me. It was wonderful. I actually got to know him as a person that night. One book was of pictures and articles about the Pacific campaign during World War II. I scoured that thing and asked my uncle questions about what it was like to be there, in the South Seas. He told me of the heat and the bugs and the constant sound of gunshot. He told me of the drinking that went on, how they'd make their own "brew." Suddenly, I came across a picture of my Uncle T: a young man, shirtless and smiling, standing on a beach on some faraway island. A picture from a time I knew nothing about but a time that came alive for me that night, sitting with my uncle and listening to his war stories. He asked me to hand him that picture of himself on that beach and suddenly he started crying. I'll never forget that moment spent with him, realizing that somewhere along the way that young handsome Irishman got lost in life. He wiped his eyes and handed the picture back to me. "Time to put the scrapbooks away." So, I did as he said, but it was a moment that I've never forgotten and the moment when I realized how much I loved this man and how I felt totally safe being with him, drunk or sober. I knew that my uncle would never hurt himself or me while I was there. He fell asleep and I went downstairs and waited for someone to come home before I left. Another night, my mother was talking with my uncle and she told me that I should go to my aunt's house because my uncle was alone and something didn't feel right to her. I went and not thinking, I opened the front door. As I did, my aunt and my cousins were screaming and yelling something fierce. They were coming up from the cellar and carrying my Uncle T. to the couch. When they saw me, my one cousin yelled for me to get out and shut the door. I ran right out, but as I was leaving I noticed that my uncle had a rope around his throat. I froze. The next moment, my cousin saw me looking at my uncle, and he slammed the door in my face. I never told my mother what I saw but at some point she had talked with my Aunt A. and told me that I didn't have to go back to their house if I didn't want to, but that I had to realize that my Uncle T. had some serious problems and when he drank that he could lose control and that was why they would send me to be with him, because they knew how much he loved me and that he wouldn't do anything if I was there. That night, they were a little slow in taking his threat of suicide seriously and he almost succeeded. His family wasn't there. I wasn't there. The terrible thing about that is you're involving a child in a situation that is way over their head and by telling them the circumstances, you scare the hell out of them and give them a terrible sense of responsibility regarding that person's life. Seeing what my uncle had done that night terrified me because I realized that he could die at any moment and he had meant so much to me, I told myself that I had to keep guard for him and make sure that he never did anything like that again. Hey, what did I know? I was all of what, 14? I only knew that I loved him and couldn't figure out why he would want to kill himself. I was too young to have noticed the disappointment he held toward his own children, or toward his failed marriage, or even toward himself. Shortly after the cellar episode one night my uncle was arguing with my cousin, his daughter. It was something stupid, some form of rebellion on her part. While arguing, my uncle suffered a heart attack. His family had a history of heart disease and it would eventually kill all but one of his brothers. He was taken to the hospital and we had to wait two days before we were allowed to see him. Again, how vulnerable and human these men seemed to me when they were ill. We were alone; my cousin was sitting out in the hall, and my uncle motioned for me to sit on the bed next to him. He took my hand and smiled at me. He seemed so weak and tired. He told me not to worry, that he was feeling much better and the one thing that he would like was some of my mother's homemade chicken soup. My Uncle T. loved my mother's chicken soup. Whenever he was sick, the order came for my mother to make a pot of soup for my uncle. That was all he would ask for. He hated my aunt's cooking. And so, my mother would make a pot of soup for him. I told him that I would get him her soup because he made me promise. He was on a restricted diet, but he wanted my mother's chicken soup. I promised I would bring it back for him. Well, walking home with my cousin, I told him that his father wanted some soup. NO WAY. He couldn't have it. I went home and told my mother and that he wasn't allowed to have it and I didn't know what to do because I had promised my uncle that I'd bring back the soup. She told me not to worry about it, that my uncle probably wouldn't remember asking for it and that he would have to focus on getting better and she'd make it for him when he came home. But, I promised him. Well, two days later, the phone rang. It was my Aunt A., screaming for my mother. My Uncle T. had a massive heart attack and died. Do you know that for years I couldn't forgive myself for not having brought him that soup. And again, before he died, I kept dreaming of him in his coffin. I kept telling my mother that something was going to happen to him but she didn't want to hear anymore about my "dreams," that he was going to be fine. Okay. I was a wreck because not six months before, my grandfather had died. I couldn't lose my Uncle T., as well. But, lose him I did. Another funeral to dread. And, the people. Biggest funeral I've ever seen. So many people loved him. I can still see him in his coffin. He was only 43 when he died.

I felt as if the two men I loved most as a kid had deserted me. I wanted to be with them, not here with everybody else. I wanted to be with them, period. I know that I will see them again.

I have held onto that thought since I was 14 years old and kept them alive since in my heart.

People tend to find this part of my story amusing. I don't know why, but they do. A significant person, another angel in my life, I consider to be Judy Garland. Go ahead, laugh if you will, but it's true. I can still remember the first time I heard that glorious voice. As a kid, I never made the connection between the album that my mother would play, with Dorothy of "Oz" fame. You see I was drawn to Judy Garland even before I knew I was gay. It wasn't her acting, it wasn't the "Oz" connection, and it certainly wasn't her infamous lifestyle. It was that voice. Hearing it, one was listening to life itself unfold. It held the entire range of emotions; joy, heartache, anger, failure, rejection, love; all the pathos referred to by the Greeks, the things that make us human. Our emotions. She was an open wound, constantly healing. I'm not all that crazy about the "Oz." Or, "A Star Is Born." I enjoy Judy Garland's films where she got to play a woman her age, living in her own time. "The Clock" stands out, as does "Presenting Lily Mars." For a display of her comic genius as well, "In the Good Old Summertime" is a classic, and the only film at MGM to turn a profit in 1948. And, there are scenes from "I Could Go on Singing," her final film that are on par with nothing else ever filmed. What a shame she wasn't in better form when making that movie. It could have been a classic. Her scene in the emergency room with Dirk Bogarde should be shown in every known film/acting class in existence. It cannot be compared. It stands alone, as did she. The day she died is burned into my memory. The same time I lost my grandfather and uncle, Judy Garland died. I sat there, newspaper in my lap, not believing what I was reading. She was gone. For years and years afterward, I would tell people about the magic and wonder of that incredible human being and they would laugh it off, telling me what a has-been she was, blah, blah, blah. Never anything about her talent, always about her personal life. To me, that was her business. I have lived long enough to see that woman's career re-emerge, as she often did, to show the world what real talent is all about.

Even after 30+ years since her death, she is still selling and still stands alone in the entertainment industry. No one compares with her; not Streisand, not LaBelle. Not even her own daughter, Liza, can stand next to her when it comes to pure talent and her ability to entertain. She LIVED her life, no matter how. She faced every challenge presented to her and when knocked down, got right back up and kept going. Through many moments in my life, and especially the darkest, she was there. I have almost always looked to her and thought, "Hell, this is nothing. I'll be fine." Here's to you, Judy, and thank you for the countless moments of sheer pleasure you have given me throughout my life.

Chapter Ten

"You Get One Mother in This Life, Only One"
Anne Bancroft in "Torch Song Trilogy"

This is going to be a tough one to write, but without it, the rest of the story sort of loses its guts, our lives were that intertwined. My mother and her story appear periodically throughout the telling of this tale, so this will be short and give you some specifics about her life, as I remember them.

She was born to Italian immigrant parents in Pennsylvania, coal-crackin' country, as I call it. My mother came from a family of ten siblings and a whole lot of drama. Her uncle committed suicide right in front of her when she was a little girl by putting a gun into his mouth at my grandmother's house and blowing out his brains. When her grandparents were visiting, if you smiled, her grandfather would slap you across the face. As a child, she was sickly so my grandmother dressed her in white to ward off the "evil eye" that had been put upon my mother. Italians, what can I say? I should take you back another step to my grandmother's life. What a wonderful creature she was. A devout Catholic, my grandmother's childhood was one of torture. To punish my grandmother, my great-grandfather would hang her by her thumbs in the basement. She was married with children and her father would still come to her home and slap her across the face, if he felt that she needed it. And they wondered why she died from a stroke at the age of 50. But, in spite of it all, my grandmother was a very loving and compassionate woman. Her sister, Angela, died after giving birth to her youngest child. My grandmother, herself having had her 9th baby, took in her sister's children, baby and all, and raised them. Apparently, their father had no use for them until they were of working age. He would come and get them and make them work, taking their paychecks. My grandmother also had second sight. Psychic, precognitive, call it what you want. She was gifted that way. If someone was ill, my grandmother would take a piece of their clothing and go to her room where she would pray and say the rosary for hours, day after day, until they were healed. Usually, it worked. The other person would get better, but my grandmother would be laid up for days, sick as a dog. My mother grew up, living in church. Every morning they walked to mass. No excuses. And of course, there was the annual novena which was across town. Nothing to do but walk every day from their home to the monastery. The walk was their penance. But my mother and her siblings grew up in a loving home. My mother would tell me wonderful stories of her childhood and teen years, growing up during the depression and World War II. I gather that her later life seemed rather anticlimactic after all of that.

In most ways, ours was a typical, Italian-American childhood, patterned after what my mother knew best. My mother's first husband was an alcoholic and she always claimed that she did not love him when he asked her to marry him and he knew it, but she felt that she would grow to love him. Never happened. My mother had two daughters by him, my older half-sisters, and in the midst of this nightmare of a marriage, she met my father and they fell in love. What does one do?? To compound matters, she became pregnant with this man's child (Hi!!). As the story goes, she tried everything she could think of to abort me. She fell down the steps, she sat in ice water baths, and she drank concoctions that almost killed her, but didn't seem to faze me. I kept growing in her tum-tum. Things were getting desperate and time was a-passing. She decided to have sex with her husband and claim that the baby was his. Ya think?? My mother walked through a snow blizzard to get across the bridge to the hospital in time for the delivery. Told you I came from strong peasant stock. I was delivered, the doctor handed me to my mother and she refused me, crying, "I wanted a daughter. Sons will leave you. Sons always leave you." So she claimed was her reaction to seeing me. Off to the nursery I went. No bonding that night. She had to come up with a name... Okay, she claimed that I was named after her father, but it was my biological father's name as well, so that covered that one. M. was her husband's name, so she can claim his part in this mess as being primary my middle name was M., and of course we'll nail B. on the end of this and really seal the deal. On January 24, 1955, JMB was born. And so, like it or not, mother's little mistake was taken home. I was not a welcomed addition to the family. My mother had confided in her best friend, who felt it then to be HER duty to inform my mother's husband of the truth. My infant years consisted of my mother going to work and her husband drinking at home and lifting me by any available appendage from my crib and smacking me senseless. I know this because my sisters used to tell me how they would fight with him to get me away from him, or how they would take me to a neighbor's house before he came home from work so I wouldn't get beaten. I am told that I was a very quiet baby, until my mother would get dressed for work, when I would start screaming. Even then, I was able to associate her leaving with the pain that would follow. Guess it didn't take long for me to figure that one out. Of course, she knew what was happening, she could see the marks he left on me, but she couldn't do anything about it. People might find out the "truth." My real father had not abandoned me. No, no. He used to sneak over or they would meet in town and he would hold me and tag along with my mother while she was shopping, begging her to leave her husband. It took my mother four years to make up her mind and my real father waited for us. I can't even imagine the beatings that I took from Mr. B. during that time, but the day came when my mother left him. You know, I can recall moving in with my real father. I remember him putting me on his shoulders and walking me through the house. He was so happy. I had my father's undivided attention for a year. For one year, I knew love. My mother then gave birth to my younger sister, and that was the end of that. He had room in his heart only for her. Now, the easy thing to do would have been to set me down and tell me the truth about my real father, right? No. Not my mother. Scandal. NO. No changing names, nothing like that. We have to keep the lie going. So, she took Mr. B. to court and sued him for child support. The utter gall of the woman. But she did it. As someone I know says, "Green is green." My mother insisted that Mr. B. treat me as one of his offspring, which meant that I was to go to him with my report cards; I was to go to him when I needed money for clothes or shoes for school, etc. I can remember those trips in the car to see "Dad." When we got there, he never looked at me, and my mother always made ME ask him for the money. I'll never forget how he'd turn around and take it out of his wallet and hand it to me. I don't know why, but I always felt so ashamed when I'd have to ask him for money and he'd turn away from me to get it. Mr. B. would come to our house every Saturday afternoon to pick up my sisters and take them out for the day. My mother would dress me and make me sit in the foyer at the front door, waiting for him. He came every Saturday, and walked right past me, got my sisters, and walked right back out the door. Can you imagine what that can do to a child's psyche, to have him sit there every Saturday, waiting, only to be left behind? And I did this every Saturday for years. Such was my mother's determination that no one know the truth, that she was willing and took part in the twisting of her own son's psyche and the distortion of my sense of self. Is it any wonder how I ended up loving a man like Jackson? Not to me. My sisters are not blameless in this nightmare, either. Far from it. Actually, their abuse is what I remember most. I have come to believe that they vented on me their frustration at being taken away from their father and family life and having my father thrust upon them. My oldest sister by six years was and still is a rather hefty thing. She would sit on me while her sister who is five years older than me would sit on my legs. The oldest would put a pillow over my head so no one could hear my screams and sit on it while the two of them proceeded to beat me. The second oldest had a "trick" she liked pulling on me when I was a toddler. She would stand at the top of the steps with my bottle and call for me, to only knock me down the steps as I reached for the bottle. Her other claim to fame was to hold me over the upstairs banister by my ankles, threatening to drop me. And this was my childhood. I never fought back. When this is what you grow up with day after day, it becomes the norm. You know nothing else. And yet, they were my family and I loved them. No matter what has happened through the years involving my family, I have always loved them. It didn't seem to mean a rat's ass to any of them, but I did. I love my sisters, always will. I love their children. I should, I helped raise them.

My mother always used to say, "One mother can take care of 100 children, but 100 children cannot take care of one mother." The truth. Here is the perfect place to tell you exactly what I mean about taking charge and living your life. At crucial moments in your life, you can actively make a change in the course of events, if it is important enough and you know in your bones that something is wrong but can be corrected. It is a time when you can either sit back feeling helpless as a situation progresses or, you can become an active participant and help shape what is taking place and make it better. More than likely, you will not receive any credit for what you have done and you may end up being hated by those you love. But for the results you may achieve, it is worth the risk involved.

After I had been given a year to live, I focused on taking care of my mother and getting her through her illness to whatever waited for her. Why? For several reasons. She was my mother. No matter what our relationship had been, she was my mother. She was dying. A disease was robbing her of all her dignity. I refused to let her end her days in a nursing home. Had it been one of us, she would have done the same. That is what being a family means. It is this simple. There are some things in life, very important things, and you only get one shot at doing them right. One of them is when your mother is dying. I think that most people find a loved one's dying so insurmountable because it is all about the other person. In order to take care of the dying person and meet <u>their</u> needs, you have to get beyond yourself and first think of them. For most, that is the hardest part. I clicked into that mode the moment my mother was diagnosed with Alzheimer's. It was no longer about me, or Jackson, or his daughter, his career or, my health. None of that mattered. Only my mother. And, it is just as amazing to see what a mother's illness can do to her children.

Another reason I wanted to take care of my mother was that I knew how my sisters would react. Funny, but when my mother was well and still working, my sisters wanted her to live with them. Of course, a source of cash, a built-in babysitter. Ah, but once she was diagnosed; now that cast a different hue. Some of these incidents have been told before, but they bear repeating here.

My youngest sister never saw our mother again. She "borrowed" my mother's car one day and that was the last we saw of it, and her.

My second oldest sister divided my mother's furniture and belongings between herself and my aunts. For once though, I got what I wanted. I got to take mom home with us.

My oldest sister told me that I could take mom to live with us, if I let her continue to receive my mother's social security check. I told her she could take whatever she wanted, I wanted mom.

I immediately closed down her credit cards which really upset my sisters. I guess that they thought the "line of credit" would continue, I don't know. But, none of it surprised me. As I tell people, I didn't grow up with my sisters; I survived growing up with my sisters.

The Thanksgiving following my mother's diagnosis, she spent with my sisters in Pennsylvania. Everything was set. Suddenly, she didn't want to go, begged me not to take her. She said that she knew she would not come back. At that point, I was exhausted from working and taking care of her every day and I needed a break. My sisters wanted her home for Thanksgiving. That's how it always was; you went to them, they didn't come to you. So, Jackson and I discussed it and decided to drive her there and pick her up after Christmas. A nice, long break. Right. I knew my sisters better than that. I planned on Thanksgiving and left it at that. She barely made it through Thanksgiving.

The first week in December, my oldest sister called and told me that they had to take mom to the emergency room, something was wrong and they weren't sure what. Tests later showed that she was having "mini-strokes" brought on by the Alzheimer's. I knew she was having them. You could see it happening. One day, while my mother and I were folding laundry, she lost all control of her hands. She became very scared and I sat her down at the kitchen table and told her that her arthritis was kicking up and this was what would happen, and not to be afraid, because she was with Jackson and me and we would help her. The one thing I learned was if I could stay calm and explain things to her, she calmed down. It wasn't easy. She had been a nurse for over 30 years. I had to think quickly. So, to Pennsylvania to see my mother. My "break" lasted a week.

I'll never forget walking into that hospital room. She didn't even look like my mother. She was so frustrated and upset. The strokes had restricted her ability to speak. Everything was garbled and/or gibberish, so no one could figure out what she wanted or was trying to say and no one bothered to try and figure it out. My older sisters told me that we had to come because she was dying. She had lost a lot of weight and had another stroke after being admitted to the hospital. I figured, "We'll see about that." One thing my mother had always been was a survivor. She would die when she was ready to die. Nobody else was calling that shot but mom.

What I saw that day in the hospital room was an absolute mess. I walked into her room and had to lean against the wall for support. Out of sheer frustration, she had pulled out clumps of her hair. She had ripped off her fingernails and dug at the cuticles until they were infected and bleeding. She had chewed her lips until they were cracked and swollen, and dug at her face with her jagged fingernails until her face bled. And no one had done anything to prevent any of this from happening. I couldn't believe what I was seeing. That her doctor, a staff of nurses and aides, and my family, could all walk into her room day after day, and not do something to help her. As soon as she saw me, she started to wail and I remembered how she had begged me not to bring her home and I wouldn't listen. I held her hands, looked into her eyes and told Jackson, "She isn't dying from anything but neglect." That was all it took. Do you remember Shirley McLaine in "Terms of Endearment"? When she asked for her daughter's pain shot and went ballistic all over those nurses at the desk? That was me. That was how I became an active participant in the events surrounding me and made a difference. And everyone hated the sight of me, but I didn't give a damn. I was there to save my mother from these idiots. My own doctor hates the sight of me because I question everything she recommends. Doctors hate a patient that becomes actively involved in their own care and treatment; however, I learned the hard way. Once, a specialist recommended a new medication and I did as he said. A week later, I ended up hemorrhaging and being ambulanced to the hospital where I spent five days getting multiple transfusions. All because of his stupid recommendation that I did NOT question. You only get one shot at that sort of thing, folks. Pay attention and question!! I was not going to let the same thing happen to my mother.

I lived at that hospital and they didn't know what hit them. Believe me, I am not my sisters. Starting that day, I went out to the nurse's station and I told the clerk to page my mother's doctor and to let me know as soon as he arrived and I wanted the charge nurse in my mother's room, now. I became Joan Crawford and nobody was going to fuck with me when it came to my mother's welfare.

You must remember that I come from an area where the general population is thought of and treated like village idiots. They are brow-beaten, discouraged from furthering themselves. It is and always has been a pit of corruption and the locals are kept dumb and drunk so that the powers that be will have a source of cheap labor, generation after generation. Not a happy place to be. I was usually in trouble of one kind or another, because I used my brain. I looked up. A very interesting thing I've noticed over the years; having come from a factory town, I have noticed that people, who live in factory towns, mill towns, mining towns, etc., rarely look UP when they walk. They tend to look down. It comes from being brow-beaten, from surrendering early in life to the inevitable rhythm of your life that will lead you to that factory and home again at the end of your shift. That is the rhythm of life in a factory town, broken only by drinking. Why educate your work force? They'll think and want more. Keep them dumb and drunk. And this was the mentality I was forced to deal with when I went back for that holiday season in Pennsylvania.

As I said, I moved into the hospital and slept in a chair in my mother's room. I met with her nurses, physicians, and with my sisters, who sat and smiled while I told the doctor he was an idiot. Here, he had a stroke patient who couldn't speak and had difficulty with swallowing, but was receiving a tray of regular food. Three times a day they brought in the tray, left it expecting her to feed herself, and three times a day came back and picked up a tray of uneaten food, and no one could figure out how she had lost almost 30 pounds.

I told him to order her a puree diet, to place intake and output sheets to monitor her liquids because she was certainly dehydrated at this point which I proved by pinching the skin on her hand and watched it tent up, and to throw an IV in her to re-hydrate her cells. He looked at me, staring blankly. I said, "Now, get out. I am going to talk with my sisters, and take that nurse who apparently hasn't even bothered to come in and comb my mother's hair, never mind check her vital signs, with you."

I then turned on my sisters.

"You idiots! She isn't dying! She's being neglected by all of you!" "Now, J..." "Don't you 'Now J' me! You act as if you want her to die. Do you have ANY common sense between you?? How could you leave her day after day, looking like this? She's a mess. I am staying here and I am going to take care of her myself." My sisters, the bitches of Eastwick as I call them, shuffled out, not to return while I was there. No one came while I was there. I let no one in, and I was almost too late in helping my mother.

I realized after a couple of days that my mother hadn't had a bowel movement. At about that time, she spiked a very high fever and lapsed into a coma. Her doctor asked if he could talk with me and we discussed what might be happening. I told him that I wanted a GI consultation and he ordered it. A well-known specialist in the area did the consult. The village idiot routine again.

"There is really nothing more we can do for your mother." "Doctor, before you submit your bill for having done absolutely nothing, I want you to order enemas-until-clear." "Why would I do that?" "Because, she hasn't had a bowel movement in almost a week." "Yes?" "You idiot. If for nothing else, to re-hydrate the lining of her bowels." That took care of him, but he ordered the enemas. She had three enemas and after everyone thought that I was crazy and being too demanding, 24 hours later the enemas kicked in and they thought her bowels would never stop producing. It kept coming. And I sat there, ringing the intercom every time and smiled, watching those lazy idiots keep cleaning her, the same people who said they were wasting their time giving her the enemas.

That night, my mother's temperature began to drop and the next day, she opened her eyes and could speak again. I'll never forget that moment. I was sitting next to her bed, when she opened her eyes and looked at me and I knew she recognized me.

She said, "You're always here. It's always you." I thought I would die. Talk about an early Christmas present. I ran out and told the nurse to call her doctor. I went back into her room and called my sisters. I told them what had happened and gave my mother the phone and she talked with them. You have to realize that because of the Alzheimer's and the mini-strokes, my mother's ability to converse was quickly deteriorating and after this stroke, her speech was totally garbled. However, now she made total sense. It was as if she woke up and had landed in a part of her brain unaffected by the disease or the strokes. It only lasted about an hour or two, and then she started slipping back. I could see the Alzheimer's pulling her back in, bit by bit, until by that night she couldn't speak coherently. But, I made sure that my sisters and Jackson talked with her before she left us again. I would remember what she said to me for years after. There was something in the way she looked at me when she said, "It's always you," that hit a strange chord and wouldn't leave me, until many years later, when the true meaning of that statement suddenly came to me and only then did her words and expression make sense. You see, I finally realized that my mother kept expecting it to be her daughters, the ones she had "helped" through all the years of their lives, only they were now too busy to help her. That's one reason it was always me. Another is that I loved her more than myself. She was my mother.

After my mother came to live with us in Massachusetts, her health deteriorated quickly, to the point that she had become bedridden and lost the ability to swallow. Her doctor talked with me and told me that there was nothing else they could do and that I was now keeping her alive more so because I couldn't let her go. She had a feeding tube, but it would only do so much. I listened to him and went home to think it over, realizing that he was right. I was refusing to believe that mom was more than ill, that she was dying and I was hindering the process. Jackson and I discussed the situation and we agreed that mom should go on hospice care. However, I refused to have aides or nurses coming in to take care of her. I took a leave of absence from work and I took care of her myself. That always seemed to surprise people, the fact that my mother had three daughters but it was her son who took care of her when she was dying. To me, it was an honor. I worshiped her. I would have done anything for her, as I know she would have done for us, her children.

The master bedroom was large enough to accommodate a hospital bed and that is where it went. I moved our bed into the study off the bedroom. That way, I could be with her 24-7. I moved the desk and loveseat from the study into the master bedroom and was with her every day and night. With the phone and TV installed, I had no reason to leave until Jackson came home after work. He would sit with her while I made dinner. My day was pretty much the same schedule every day. I would wash her every morning and change her gown and sheets, give her fluids via her feeding tube to keep her hydrated. Being on hospice care, she was not allowed any solids, only hydration. Her diet consisted of water and juices throughout the day. All of her medications had been stopped and she had been placed on morphine via the PEG tube. The nurses came in every other day to monitor her care and vital signs. This went on for six weeks. And for six weeks, I never left her side. I know that Jackson became concerned because of my own health issues, but at that time nothing else mattered to me. I said, there are some things in life where you get one chance to get it right. Don't screw it up.

My older sisters came for a visit but turned out to be more of a hindrance. My oldest sister spent most of her time trying to track down her husband's whereabouts while she was away. She refused to help take care of mom, even though she had worked in a nursing home and knew how to give patient care. No way was she going to touch her. My older sister would sit there telling mom to look for the white light, that it was her time to go. After a few days of this, I threw them both out. I told them that I wanted them both to go in and make their peace with mom and leave, so she could die in peace. They were not happy with my decision, but I had had enough of it being about them. I did not want to argue, I wanted them to leave. Of course, being my sisters, they asked if they could take my mother's personal belongings with them. I told them to take whatever they wanted, but to leave. With their appetites sated and car fully packed, they were gone within the hour. They even took mom's false teeth! Family. I went to my mother's room. I thanked God that earlier, before their arrival, she had slipped into a coma. This way she did not have to deal with her daughters and their petty greed.

My sisters left on Wednesday. My mother passed away on Friday. Leave it to her to die after they left. She knew what was going on. My mother captained her own ship. That is why my diagnosis became secondary. Helping my mother became the focus of my attention. I would deal with my illness and my demons later. As we say in the Lord's Prayer, "Thy will be done."

Chapter Eleven

An Aside, if You Will

How in God's name do you describe a miracle? You have to begin at the beginning. And, as it is an integral part of this story, I need to tell you about it. That I am aware of, it encompassed 11 years of my life, in active form; from 1993 to 2004. The miracle itself was of only a moment's time, but I was aware of it when it happened. Want to go back with me?

In 1993, I went to my doctor for a routine physical. I had been in France with Jackson and had come back. I had applied for a job at a local hospital and went in for the necessary blood work and physical exam. The next day they called and told me that I needed to see my doctor and that they had faxed the blood work results to her and she would discuss them with me. Hmm...something's not right. So, I called and her partner told me to come in that day, that my doctor was not in but that she would see me and yes, she had gotten the blood work results. Hmm...now I know something's not right. I went to her office, where she had more blood drawn. She sat down with me and told me that my hepatitis B had gone from passive to active. This was not good news. She told me that there was nothing that could be done but that my doctor would be in the following day and she would discuss the results with her, as well as the results of that day's blood work. And, that was that. She was very nice but not very helpful. Amazing, isn't it?? How they tell you something so catastrophic and then let you go, not knowing what you might do to yourself. It was late in the day as I remember it and I was so shocked, I didn't know where to go, what to do, or even what to think. I knew that I felt fine. I felt somewhat tired, but not having experienced symptoms prior to this, I had no idea that it was a symptom of liver disease. I could only wait and talk with my doctor the following day. That was probably the longest all-nighter I have ever pulled. Just stared at the ceiling all night long, wondering what the hell was going to happen to me. Remember, this was before my fateful meeting with Nelson, the psychic. I wasn't even aware of his existence at that time in my life. That was yet to come.

As it happened, my mother was staying with me. Before any of this news, we had decided that she would come and stay with us in Rochester. I had also decided to take her to a local hospital that specialized in geriatric medicine and have her tested, as I had noticed when she arrived that her behavior was somewhat flighty and forgetful. Even stranger, the first appointment that they had available was on my birthday. January 24th. Being Italian, I took this as a good omen. My suspicion had been that since she had been taking Valium for so many years, it was time to wean her. Jesus in heaven, where were my brain cells that day. Anyway, I went home after the doctor's discovery, and spent the time with my mother. I wanted to forget about my illness. I couldn't discuss it with her. When I got back home and saw her, I made the decision to never tell her about my illness. What good would it have done? I knew that something was wrong with my mother and I wasn't about to add to her problems. My sisters couldn't or wouldn't see that there was a problem, but as soon as I saw her again, I knew. So, we made dinner and talked and watched television and I passed the time as best as I could without jumping out of my skin. I remember getting out of bed around midnight and going into my mother's room. I woke her and sat on the bed, telling her that after spending so much time with Jackson in France that I couldn't adjust to sleeping alone again and I asked her if I could sleep on the floor in her bedroom. My mother being my mother told me, "Yes, and bring your rosary with you. Something's wrong and since you won't tell me, we're going to say the rosary together." That was my mom. So, rosary in hand, I went back into her room and threw a pillow and blanket onto the floor, and we proceeded to say the rosary together. I was out in about 20 minutes. The rosary is an amazing thing. I'll always say that. Plus the fact that I wasn't alone. That was as great a help to me that night.

The next day, I went to see my doctor. Dr. Kirn, a wonderful woman. I have never again experienced the feeling of having a physician totally on my side during my battle with my illness, as I had with Dr. Kirn. She was a storm trooper when it came to our approaching this disease. An amazing person. She told me that for some inexplicable reason, the virus had gone active.

People who have been infected with the hepatitis B virus break into several categories, or did so at that time. First, there is the majority whose bodies fight the virus and develop antibodies. Then there's the unfortunate group who die. Then there's the strange group whose bodies, for whatever reason, don't recognize the virus as a threat, and they are known as "carriers." The virus is of no danger to them but it can be passed on to others through the carrier's semen or blood. In many ways, like the A.I.D.S. virus, and can be as deadly. I was classified as a carrier. The virus lay dormant within my body; a co-existence, if you will.

Dr. Kirn sent me to a specialist to see what was happening. He in turn had blood work done and then scheduled a liver biopsy. He performed that at a local hospital and we then waited for the results. My liver biopsy was scheduled for the same day Jackson was to be in Massachusetts to start his new job. I did not ask him to stay and he did not offer. God gave me the sign but I chose to ignore it. I don't think I'm being selfish in saying or thinking that; it was not discussed. Not how I was getting there, getting home, how I would recover, if there might be complications, nothing. He was focused on his new job and left my problems up to me, and as always, I handled everything. Oddly enough, my former partner took me, stayed at the hospital and then took me home. He called to make sure that I was all right and to see if I needed anything, not Jackson.

Two days after the procedure I was back in the specialist's office. He asked if someone came with me and I told him no, that I was alone. He proceeded to tell me that I had extensive fibrotic tissue (Meaning cirrhosis) and about 10% of my liver was functioning. I showed no symptoms, was not jaundiced or in any pain. The only symptom was my blood work. Everything was haywire. Values that should have been in the 30-70 range were in the 700's. Everything was totally out of whack. And, there was no medication available at the time, other than Interferon, but my case was too far advanced. They surmised that because of the extent of the cirrhosis, I had the hepatitis B virus for at least 15-20 years and wanted to know how I may have become exposed at an early age; possibly as a teenager. I could only think of when I had been raped and remembered a conversation with my sister when she told me that the relative who had raped me was in the hospital because of problems with his liver several years before and his needing a biopsy and it turning out to be a hepatitis B related infection and that he may have needed a transplant. Suddenly, it all came back. All the years of suppression of anger and denial of the rape were there before me again.

I actually felt sorry for the doctor because he had nothing to offer as for help. I stood up and said, "Doctor there is nothing you could tell me that would be more devastating to me than hearing my mother's diagnosis of Alzheimer's. I have to focus right now on taking care of her and making sure that she will be all right if something should happen to me. Goodbye, and thank you."

Honestly, I've only ever had one episode and that was shortly after my mom passed away, where I hemorrhaged and was rushed to the hospital at U. Mass. I was not even aware that I was bleeding. I had prayed to my mother to give me a sign that I was not going through all of this alone, that she was with me. Well, I had received several pints of blood, was admitted, and the following day went for an upper endoscopy. The specialist told me that I had a duodenal ulcer the size of Idaho. Afterward, the secretary was going to lunch and asked if I would take my chart back to the floor with me when the volunteer arrived to take me back to the ward. I said I would. When she left, I looked through my chart (How often does a patient get to look at their chart??). On the face sheet I saw my name, address, etc. As I scanned the sheet reading the information, I came to the line "In case of emergency, notify..." and there I stopped, not able to believe what I was seeing. It listed my mother's name. I never listed my mother. It was always Jackson's name that I used. I started crying as I remembered that the night before while receiving the transfusion, I had prayed to mom. I now knew that she had heard my prayers. I went back to the floor and asked the unit clerk how they received the information for the face sheet and she told me it was a computer printout. I then told her what had happened and that I was ready to go home. My doctor came up and was amazed at how well I looked and agreed that I could leave.

A week later I went back for a follow-up endoscopy. Afterward, the specialist asked to look at the former endoscopy report and films. When he came back, he looked very frustrated, so I asked what was wrong. He told me that not only had the ulcer completely healed but that there was no scarring any where. There was no indication that I had a duodenal ulcer at all, ever. I told him about my mother and I felt that since she had been a nurse for so many years helping others, that what she could not do for me while she was alive, she could do now from the other side. I thanked him and left. This was the "miracle". You see, the doctor told me that I should have died during the drive to U. Mass. in the ambulance. But, my body and the virus made some sort of truce. So what happened was that instead of following through with the dying process of hemorrhaging, shock from the massive loss of fluids and then death, the virus backed off and has remained in what the doctor described as a "sentinel" position, just watching and waiting. From that time, my body and the virus have basically had a co-existence; each recognizing the other, but not doing a damn thing about conquering or killing. That is what stumps the doctors.

And, in 13 years, that is the only episode I have ever had dealing with my liver, an episode Nelson foresaw and warned me about. I have seen specialists in Rochester, Massachusetts, Seattle, Buffalo, everywhere I have lived including France, and they have all agreed on one point; I should be dead. I finally had to admit to myself that for some unknown reason, I am meant to live.

It is a terrible feeling of guilt one carries when you are taking care of someone else who is dying, knowing that it should be you in that bed and it isn't. One thing I never understood about my being terminally ill and not dying is that not one doctor ever looked at me and said, "What is so different about you that you are still alive? I would like to study you." I would think that a lot could be learned from my case; however, as a friend of mine who is a doctor stated, "You defy all medical knowledge written on this disease. You are the exact opposite of what we study in medical school. Doctors will avoid you because you are outside the realm of their knowledge". I would think that to be the **exact** reason they would want to study my case. I am an example to show patients that it may not be a death sentence for them. My case would give them hope, but I've never been able to get a doctor to see it that way. It bothers me a great deal that there are people out there given this terminal diagnosis every day and their mindset becomes that of a dying person, when if they could change that mind set it could save their lives, or make dying less fearful for them. I wish in my lifetime that I could make that happen. Just that and I would know my life had meaning and I was able to help even one person through dealing with the nightmare of this type of diagnosis. Maybe telling this story will help someone. And, what is the secret to surviving this type of diagnosis? For me, it was to get involved in something bigger than my own life's issues. And so, I focused on taking care of my mother and helping her get through the ravaging effects of Alzheimer's disease. And, I did not allow her illness or death to become stresses in my life. After my initial diagnosis, I rid myself of as much stress in my life as I could. I really do believe that stress is the major killer in our society. I dumped whatever I found to be stressful. Also, I held nothing back. My opinions were out there. I tell people even now, if you don't want the truth don't ask for my opinion. For years my sisters told their children, "If you want the truth, ask your uncle. If you can't handle the truth, don't bother asking him." I became that way because I realized how valuable and precious our time here really is. It has not been easy. I have lost friends, jobs, family, and even partners because I am so direct. Cut the bullshit out of your life and start living! That's my motto. You don't have to be cruel, but be honest.

Dr. Kirn wanted to know what I had done in France that may have caused the virus to go active. Well, how about the fact that as soon as I arrived, Jackson told me that he was having an affair with a woman at work and wanted to break up with me and marry her? Plus the fact that my mother had recently been diagnosed with Alzheimer's?? And how about my being given a year to live?? Would the shock and stress of all of that have caused the virus to suddenly go active?? You can bet your buns on that one. Stress is an incredibly powerful thing, and can drop you like a stone no matter how healthy and/or fit you may be. Don't fool around with stress because you will lose. I am a firm believer that stress is THE major killer in this world. No need to discuss heart disease or cancer or anything else...they are all based in some form of stress in our lives. I am living proof.

Chapter Twelve

"On A Clear Day..."
My Seer, My All

N elson. What a wonderful man. His arrival in my life was totally unexpected and by chance. A fluke of fate. But, that one session with him opened a door to my future that had it remained closed, I probably would have died or committed suicide. His words alone kept me going through the nightmare my life would become.

At the end of October 1995, Jackson and I decided to take a weekend trip to Rochester to visit friends. We were staying with my friend, Cassie, whom I had known since first moving to Rochester in 1985. She was like a sister to me. We talked every day or visited one another weekly. I loved Cassie. Both being Italian, we hit if off immediately and she loved my mother.

While we were there, Cassie told me of a psychic she had seen, his name being Nelson. She thought that with everything going on with my mom and my health issues, I should go to see Nelson. I called and left a message but never heard back from him. Our weekend progressed and finally it was time to leave. As we packed the car, the phone rang. It was Nelson. He had been out of town but was very interested in doing a reading for me. As his office was along the route we would be taking to go home, he could meet me at his office in an hour. Okay.

We said our goodbyes and headed east to Nelson's office. Once there, I went in while Jackson waited in the parking lot. This was not his idea of fun. Not my problem. In my life, between fortune tellers, readers of cards, etc., plus my being precognitive, all added up to one thing – there was more to life. For God's sake, we lived in a haunted house! I had relatives who read tea leaves and coffee grounds in cups, tarot cards. This was not new to me. And although he had plenty of his own experiences in our house with the unexplained, Jackson wanted nothing to do with the supernatural. In I went, wondering what would present itself to me through this man.

To my relief, Nelson and I hit it off immediately. He was a strikingly handsome man, older, very distinguished looking. He started by telling me to place my palm upright in front of him on the desk. He would gently tap the mounds at the bases of my fingers with his index finger while talking with me. Then, he said, "There are many here, all wanting to communicate something to you. You are much loved and thought of on the other side, J. Many wait for and watch out for you. You will have a long life." At this, I chuckled, thinking of my diagnosis. Nelson continued. "I didn't say it would be a healthy life or without problems, but considering what the doctors have told you, I wanted to reassure you that you are not going to die. Do not listen to them and you'll be fine". Now he had my full attention.

Still tapping my palm, he nodded his head as if agreeing with someone and said, "You have to listen very carefully to what I am going to tell you, J. There are five major events that are coming into your life and you have to prepare yourself for them. The first will be your mother's death. She will not live to see the new year. You plan on taking care of her at home. Do that. The spirits that reside there will help her to cross over. They will lead her to her mother. When she sees her, she will cross over. Expect no help from your family, but God has heard your request and you will be there when your mother passes on. Soon after the new year, your partner will change jobs and leave you. I see him traveling over water. You will suddenly become seriously ill and although they will expect you to die, you won't. God will intervene. Your survival will remain a mystery to your doctors. When it happens, relax and know you are being protected from harm. You will also meet a doctor, a foreigner, who will save your life. Listen to his advice. He will be a great help to you in dealing with your condition. Finally, your partner will leave you. I see his feelings for you dissipating gradually and I see him walking away from you and getting on with his own life, leaving you.

Do not concern yourself with these things right now as they will happen over a period of years; however, they will begin soon and carry on to completion with his leaving you". Again, he shook his head as if hearing something and nodding in agreement and understanding.

"I know that this is a lot to absorb all at once, but those here want you to be aware of these events so you will not be overcome by them, as you will have to deal with all of this alone. There is an Uncle T. here, with an Aunt M. and an Aunt R., and an older male, a grandfather J., who spoke with an accent, someone you loved dearly. They know you love them and they want to help you to get through all of this. J., at the end of all this devastation you will write a book which will help many, many people and at that point your mother will come back into your life and act as a guide for you to help people heal. There, they have gone."

Nelson let go of my hand and slumped back in his chair. I was speechless. I realized that almost an hour had passed without either one of us realizing. I had not moved a muscle and finally relaxed to feel how stiff I was from listening so intently.

Rubbing his eyes and coughing, Nelson sighed, "My God, that was intense. I haven't done a reading like that in years! They were seriously hell-bent on getting that information to you! You certainly have enough spirit looking out for you. J. Please, don't be afraid of anything you have been told. They wanted to prepare you because they protect and love you. You will be all right. Be ready for it and good luck. You can and will contact me in the future. Know I am here to help you as well. You have a very exciting future ahead of you. Once you work your way through this period of constant upheaval and change, your life will take off. And believe me, your partner will regret leaving you for the rest of his life. You will see and experience more than he ever thought possible. Know that you will live to stand at his grave as well. You have a lot of living ahead of you, as well as hard work. Remember, God is with you, always. Now, do you have any questions for me?"

"Questions? After that reading? I can barely remember my own name, never mind the reading! God, what will I tell Jackson? He's going to ask about our session!"

"Tell him nothing of this reading, other than of your mother's fate and his new job. Nothing else, J. Start protecting yourself and preparing for the inevitable. Why tell him what he would keep from you? Now, it is time to go home and begin your journey."

Time to begin? I was numb walking back to the car and there sat Jackson, staring at me, trying to read my face. "Well? How was it? What did he say that took so long?" Looking straight ahead and trying to not look confused, I said, "Um, he told me that mom would die before the end of the year, not to expect any help from my sisters, and that you would take another job overseas. That's all." Staring right at me, he said, "That's all...all that time and that's all?" I said, "Sort of. He talked about her illness and what would happen. He mentioned my health and the doctors. Then, he went into your leaving for Europe again. Yea, that was about it. Why, what time is it? Let's get going."

Shaking his head, Jackson pulled out of the lot. "What a crock! You were there an hour and that's all of it. Why so long? So he could charge for a full hour, I'll bet." Staring out the side window and thinking of everything that lay in wait ahead of me, I said, "Yep, that's about it, hon."

Although Nelson and I would speak many times over the phone and correspond as I traveled in search of myself, we only saw one another once more.

After my mother died and Jackson moved to Europe and I hemorrhaged, I went back to see Nelson in Rochester, telling him everything that had happened, how right he had been in his earlier predictions. Being Nelson, he listened and downplayed his part in it and then told me that my mother was here with us and had a message for me, but that she would bring it to me herself. He also warned me of a betrayal that was coming. The last thing that he told me was did I remember him telling me that Jackson would leave. I said that I did. He said to remember that Jackson would find a way to know where I was and how I was. In that sense, he would not let go. I found that an odd and scary statement to make almost like a warning, but I listened to Nelson's advice. I was staying at my friend Cassie's house and went back after the session. The next day, Cassie was home, cleaning. So, I went into the guest room and stretched out on the bed and told her about the odd message that Nelson had given me regarding my mother. Now, Cassie was standing directly outside of my room, dusting the door frame while I was lying on the bed, with the door open. I was on my side when suddenly I heard my mother's voice, telling me "Pray for her, pray for her. She will be fine. There is nothing to worry about. She needs your prayers". At first I didn't really take in the message, as I was so surprised to hear my mother's voice again. Then what was taking place sank into my psyche! I listened intently, waiting for her to tell me who needed my prayers. Suddenly, I turned over as the voice was coming from behind me. When I did, it stopped. I jumped up and yelled for Cassie. She came right in and I asked her if she had heard anything. "No, nothing. Why?" I told her about hearing my mother's voice and the message she gave me. Cassie was stunned, but swore she had heard nothing, even though she was standing outside the room. All she heard was me saying, "Who?", as I asked my mother who needed my prayers. I was flying high.

To have heard my mother's voice again was incredibly elating. I now knew life actually went on.

I left Rochester, heading back to Gardner. When I arrived home, there were several messages from a cousin of mine, in NEPA. I called her immediately to find out what she wanted. She told me that another cousin of ours had been rushed to a local medical center, as she went into multiple-organ failure. She was waiting for a heart transplant and suddenly, for no reason, her organs began shutting down. She lasted overnight and died the following morning after arriving at the medical center. It turned out that the day my mother came to Nelson with her message was the day that my cousin was rushed to the hospital. The following day, when she came to me, was the day that my cousin went into organ failure and died.

Chapter Thirteen

"Or, Am I Losing My Mind..."

I realize that I have taken you on quite a hectic journey with my bouncing around through the years. Please remember though that it has been a hectic existence for me; not as bad now, but that took work and a conscious effort on my part to change that quality in my life.

My dear friend, Carole, read this story and her comment made me realize I had chosen the right title. She said, "But Jude, it's missing your sense of humor. How will people know how funny you are?" I thought about that and told her that it was my humor that covered the pain all those years and so the story is about the pain. My humor is very evident, but my pain isn't. I now realize that the title "Missing The Laughter" goes far beyond being a comment Jackson made to his daughter. It actually carries greater personal significance. This story is my life, missing the laughter.

The four years that Jackson spent in Europe were very hectic for the both of us. Even though we were thousands of miles apart, we still had things to do and lives to live involving one another.

Jackson's time was spent working on his goal of climbing the corporate ladder which included a lot of traveling, lots of meetings anywhere in the world and taking either promotions or totally different jobs with other European firms. He became a valued commodity to European firms because of his extensive dealings negotiating contracts with American and foreign governments and their requirements for establishing facilities in their respective countries.

My time was spent primarily with keeping an eye on my mother whose health was declining, monitoring my own well being and keeping life going on the home front. Because we had such a large home, most of my time was spent working on it and the landscaping. When you have 13 rooms and three floors of living space, that can be a lot of work for one person, but it kept me busy and my mind off of my health.

My mother came to live with us when her health was deteriorating. Jackson and I talked about it and he decided to take a position stateside that would allow him to be at home and help take care of mom. I realized how close they were and I wanted him there to work through this and have closure when she died. I didn't want him to experience again what he did when his own mother died. It was the right thing to do; however, I was not expecting him to accept an assignment in Europe three weeks after she died, and leave. But, he did. And again, I dealt with whatever problems were left behind. I kept working on the house and had included a memorial garden for my mother in the landscaping which I worked on all that spring and summer. That was my way of dealing with my grief and mourning my mother's passing.

I want to share with you the day my mother died because it was a very profound and yet peaceful event and I want you to know that death needn't be filled with pain and stress. It can be a beautiful experience.

Strange as it may sound, I equate death with birth, only in reverse. Seriously, if you reverse the process in your mind, it is the same. In death, you are usually in a dark place (Such as a coma) as in birth and move on to the unknown, for you. In birth, there are unknown forces and hands guiding the journey here to welcome you. In death, unknown forces and hands guide and monitor you on. How are we to know that there aren't unknown forces waiting to welcome us. Taking a bigger leap, how can we be sure that <u>this</u> isn't death and what we go to is actually life? We can't; however, there have been enough experiences through new centuries of time for us to realize and accept that this isn't all that there is for us.

After my mother's stroke in Pennsylvania, Jackson and I brought her home. Earlier in this story I told you that Jackson had decided to take a job stateside because mom's health was deteriorating.

Gradually, she became bedridden; slowing down by the week, sometimes by the day you could notice the difference. I had posted signs on every door, telling her which room was beyond which door; however, even in big, bright print she lost her ability to decipher words and her world became smaller, eventually only her bedroom offering any sense of familiarity for her through her personal belongings and pictures all around of us, her children. Amazingly, she always recognized Jackson and me. Not being able to say our names, she would smile when we came into her room and <u>always</u> we would go to her so she could hold our faces in her hands, brush back our hair and give us two quick kisses on our foreheads – that became mom's "Hello" for the two of us – every morning and every night. I came to look forward to her little gesture. To me, that sign showed me that she was still there and still mom. I hung on to anything, any sign where I could see even a glimmer of my mother behind the nightmare. When she retreated to her bed and began having problems swallowing, her doctor talked with me and wanted me to see that her life was coming to an end and I had to stop fighting the process which had already begun and one she was dealing with and accepting, as he could see by her gradual retreat to her bedroom. He wanted me to see that it would become physically painful for her with her problems swallowing and being bedridden. So, he told me of his plan for her. He was going to order Hospice Care, place a feeding (PEG) tube to keep her hydrated and stop her medications, placing her on morphine for pain. He gave me two days to think over his plan. Two days to initiate the inevitable. How could I do this? I felt as if I was abandoning her. When Jackson came home from work, we talked about it and although I was upset by it , he agreed with the doctor and told me that I had to let go of her.

Poor Jackson. I'd had that phrase beating at my psyche all day. Finally, when he said it, something snapped. In our living room, the fireplace had floor-to-ceiling built-in bookshelves. I was standing at the fireplace and Jackson was sitting at the piano when he said, "You have got to let go of her." I turned toward him with my fists clenched and said, "That fucking phrase! I am sick to death of hearing it! Let go of her? I finally have her in my life without my damn sisters bleeding her dry with their wanting and wanting! She can finally relax and be, and <u>for what!</u> To give up and die? Is that the only time I deserve to spend with her? Is it? I get the fucking 'honor' of watching her starve and choke to death??" I turned to face the mantel and suddenly I started yelling, "**NO!!!**" and I swept everything from the mantel; silver candlesticks, antique Sheffield dogs, ivory miniature portraits; everything gone, sailing, shattering against the side wall. Jackson jumped up. "Are you crazy!!??" I stared back at him. "Am I, Jackson? Watch!!" I turned toward the bookcase. I heaved books of all sizes at every lamp and antique statue set out on the tables in the living room. I remember beaning a pair of white Italian lamps on either side of the sofa in the front bay window, shattering one of them when it hit the wood floor. All of our family pictures I had framed and placed them together on top of the piano with silver candlesticks under hurricane glass shades. Thanks to my days on the bowling league, I wiped that cluster clean with the Webster's Dictionary and an Agatha Christie autobiography for my spare shot. Jackson knew better than to say another word. He stood there with his hands over his eyes, waiting for it to end. I took a deep breath, wiping my hands on my shirt. "Wow!!! That felt great!! I feel so much better!! Don't worry, Jackson. I'll clean it all up in the morning. Now you have an excuse to go shopping for more 'guilt' presents. You know, those are the gifts I get when you have another affair. Well, now we have somewhere to put them. You see Jackson, I know you've had another affair. But, I'm telling you right now that until she draws her last breath, my mother is my main concern. Do you think until that happens you can act like a normal human being? No drama, no anxiety involving you and your job? It's going to have to be, Jackson. For once in all the years that we have been together, it is <u>not</u> going to be all about you. I don't have the time to deal with your bullshit right now. It has nothing to do with my love for you and it is not some form of punishment. That woman upstairs needs all of our attention to finish this and I intend to be there every moment so she knows she isn't alone. If you can't think beyond yourself just this once, stay the hell out of my way."

And, off I went, leaving him standing in the rubble with his jaw on the floor, wondering how I knew about his affair. When it came to that, I always knew. I'm an Aquarian.

In the morning, I went down and had my coffee, letting the cats out while I walked through the gardens with Missie at my side. I slept like a stone the night before and felt totally revived. Jackson had quietly dressed and left for work before I'd even stirred. "Better for him," I thought, as I checked out my bed of Japanese Iris and headed for the embankment where I had moved the lilac bushes, and checked the masses of black-eyed Susan's that had overtaken the slope below the lilacs. My gardens always invigorated me. Walking through or sitting on one of the hidden benches or on the canopied swing with one of the cats while waiting for the hummingbirds always seemed to focus me.

That afternoon, I called my mother's doctor and told him that he was right, that it was time to help her finish her journey here. I told him that visiting nurses were welcome to monitor her care, but I had been a certified nurse's aide and I would be taking care of her. He had no objections and told me that the nurses would instruct me in her care and administering the liquid morphine through her feeding tube.

When Jackson came home, minus any mess to be cleaned up and his usual acting as if nothing had happened after a crisis so there would be no discussing it, I told him of my plans for mom and that I was moving her bed into the master bedroom and ours into the study off of it so I would be there day and night in case she choked or needed something. He was in total agreement, which I had expected. Plus, I really wanted him to be a part of this process so he would get to say goodbye to mom.

For almost six weeks, the daily routine centered totally around mom. I took a leave of absence from work and spent my day with mom, breaking only when Jackson came home. I would go down and get dinner going while he talked with mom and changed his clothes. Coma or no coma, we treated her the same; talking with her, discussing family or what was on the news. My day started with getting her washed and changing her night gown and sheets. Every 15 minutes, I would re-position her so she wouldn't get sores. Every 30 minutes, I gave her juice and/or water in her PEG tube to keep her hydrated. Every morning, after she was washed, I gave her a rubdown and every night I massaged her feet. Three times a day, I did range-of-motion exercises on her joints. At first, Jackson had no idea what my day consisted of, until the weekend came. He was shocked. "She is dying. You're still trying to keep her alive." "Jackson, just because she is dying does not mean it has to be a painful experience for her, physically. If we were to leave her in this bed and do nothing, she would be in such pain. This way, I know that although she is dying, I am making her as comfortable as I can. I am not hindering the process, Jackson. I know she's dying. Why should it be a rough road for her?" I had the visiting nurse phone and explain to him that my care would not prevent her death, only keep her comfortable. I found myself dealing less with Jackson and more with the process of mom's dying. Eventually, I had to start using a suction tube because she lost the ability to swallow and I was not going to let her choke to death. It is a horrible way to die. Her father had died that way. It was not going to happen to her while I was there.

As you know, my sisters came and went.

One day the nurse arrived and took mom's vital signs while I stood there, watching. She looked at me and said, "Do me a favor and look at your mother. Then, tell me what you see." So, I looked at her and said, "She looks the same. Why?" The nurse said, "J, she's dying. First, look at her face. I've never seen anything like it, but your mother's wrinkles are all gone. Look at her face. Where are the wrinkles around her eyes and her mouth?" I looked again and I swear, she had not one wrinkle. All gone. She looked so peaceful. I thought, "This is how she must have looked as a young woman." "Now I'm going to show you something else." She reached over the rail and lifted my mother's hand, pinching the skin which tented up and stayed that way. "She has lost her body fluids. She is dying, J. I doubt she will last the night. I'm going to call her doctor and make him aware of this."

I was in shock. I looked at my mother and realized that I hadn't seen any of it, as if I wasn't meant to. I sat down and tried to focus, trying to adjust to the fact that she was really dying; now, instead of weeks or days, it was in hours. The nurse did the paper work involved and left around 6 p.m. I sat there, staring at her, listening to the rhythm of her breathing. Nothing seemed any different from any other day of the past six weeks. Yet, somehow, this time I knew the nurse was right. Something had changed. I went to her bed. I picked her up and held her in my arms. I told her what a wonderful mother she had been and how much I loved her and knew that I would see her again, but if she was ready to go that I understood and I wanted her to be out of pain and at peace. I kissed her and put her back down in the bed and kept my cheek on her forehead for a few minutes.

At about 7-o'clock, Jackson came home. He had his ritual of coming upstairs and talking with my mother. He would change his clothes and take the dog out for its walk while I made dinner. I couldn't tell him what the nurse had said and so, I told him that I wasn't very hungry yet, that I wanted to sit with mom for a while. He went to change and headed downstairs.

I was sitting at my desk when suddenly I heard a voice say, "Go to her, she's dying." I looked toward my mother, but nothing had changed. She was still breathing at a normal rate; however, I got up and went to her bed. I let down the side rail and sat there next to her, holding her hand, telling her how much I loved her. I remember her letting out a small puff of air and then there was total silence. I listened, waiting for her to inhale again. Nothing. I knew that she was gone. I went down to the kitchen to the back door. There stood Jackson in the yard. When he looked at me, he knew something had happened. He came in, took me by the shoulders and I said, "She's gone, Jackson." Not believing me, he ran upstairs, calling "Mom!" I went up after him. There he was, sitting in the bed, holding her in his arms, crying and crying. I went to him and gently put her back on the bed. I held him and rocked him, telling him, "I will always be grateful for how much you loved her, Jackson. She absolutely adored you. You helped make a terrible part of her life a happy time for her. She got to know and love you before this awful thing overtook her. Thank you for loving her so much, Jackson. Now, I want you to help me get her ready for the undertaker." Jackson was a bit confused, but I told him that we were going to wash her and change her clothes because they would be coming to take the body to the funeral home. Looking at me as if I were totally insane, I explained, "I did this at the nursing home when I was an aide. As a nurse, my mother did it for over 30 years. If I can do it for strangers, I can do it for my own mother, Jackson." And so, we stood together in that bedroom, washing my mother's body and telling stories about her life, even chuckling at some of her zanier moments spent with us.

Seven years after her death a thought occurred to me. When it did, I finally stopped mourning for my mother. It came to me that she was waiting for Jackson to come home before she died. She was waiting for him, not me; then she died.

One very bright spot was that Jackson's daughter came to live with me after my mother's death. She had been accepted at a major university for the following year and had decided to take some easy courses and get them out of the way while she had the time. So, she moved in and took over the third floor as her "domain" and attended a local college for two semesters. We had a great time together and really bonded that year we spent in Massachusetts. When she arrived, I was amazed at the difference! No longer the skinny kid, all arms and legs, standing there chewing on a piece of her hair with those big, searching eyes of hers. No, she had grown up while she was away from us. Now I saw a tall, long-legged beauty with those beautiful eyes smiling at me when she came into the house. She seemed so sure of herself. I suddenly felt sad, thinking that she no longer needed us. Still ready to laugh at any given moment, we were both chuckling and falling into each other's arms within minutes. I also think it was good for her because she missed my mother so much and I enjoyed talking about my mom with Jackson's daughter which helped the both of us a great deal in accepting mom's death. A startling moment came for me when she told me that she had decided to major in theatre instead of pre-law, as had been her parent's dream for her. When I asked why, she said, "It's your fault, you know. All the years I spent listening to your stories of living in New York city and studying acting, all the drives we'd take and you'd throw in a CD and explain to me how important phrasing a lyric was and make me listen to Sinatra and Garland, or you would tell me to pick a song and you would say tell me to say the lyrics out loud as if I was using them in a conversation or have me write them out to see if they held the same meaning. All of that was your doing, J. You made me realize that I wanted to study theatre when I go to New York. The pre-law dream was my parents' dream, never mine. So see? It's all your fault. My parents are not going to be very happy with you!!" As I sat there, taking all of this in, my first reaction was one of humility; it occurred to me that I had actually had an impact on her life, that she had actually been listening for all those years. It really had made a difference! I suddenly jumped up and ran to her, grabbing her and whirling her around the kitchen. "You are going to have so much fun in New York!!! Oh, it's so exciting!!!" And the rest of what she said hit me…"Oh shit!! Your parents are going to kill me!!!" We stood there looking at one another and she let out this devilish little giggle that she has and I started giggling and we both ended up on the floor laughing our asses off!! After a while, we calmed down and I said, "I want to give you just one piece of advice. Your parents are going to wait for you to fall on your face and come running to them for help. They are probably going to take that moment to prove to you how wrong you were in your choice. Sweetie, if it's what you really want, I will do everything I can at that time, if you need any help. Call me first; okay?" I would deal with Jackson if and when the time came.

And, this is how we spent the last four years of our relationship; traveling back and forth, keeping things going here so Jackson would have a home to come to and relax. When we were together, I would be a sounding board for him, letting him vent all of his frustrations and fears involved with playing the politics needed to get ahead in the corporate world. I would sit for hours, letting him vent; watching him pace the floor, or holding him when the pressures were too much and he needed to cry it all out.

I never was short with him. I never told him to get into another line of work. I never criticized him for being weak. I soothed, I calmed and I listened. Why? Because I knew that as stressful as it may have been, this work gave Jackson's life meaning for him. To criticize or worry would have only added to his stress. He needed to know that there was someone who would listen. That someone was me. Unfortunately, even after we broke up, he expected me to still be the one to listen! As they say, "Ya think?"

And, the end was at hand.

Chapter Fourteen

"What A Fool Believes..."
Doobie Brothers

T hat following January I believe is when Jackson called to
tell me that there was an opening with his company in their
American facility. It was a vice-president's position and it was
being offered to him. The culmination of our ten-year plan was
finally coming to fruition. I couldn't believe it. It had actually
worked. All that time and effort, not to mention the separations
for months at a time. That had been the toughest part. You can do
just so much from across an ocean. I was starting to show signs
of strain, as was our relationship, from being apart and making
decisions for one another thousands of miles away. Jackson and I
needed to talk about our relationship. I knew that, had known for
months. We had been to Hell and back in this relationship. Right
from the beginning, with his affairs. To me, it was a sign of his
insecurity. I felt that he didn't know how good he was at what he
did. Nothing seemed to show him how talented and valuable he
was at his job. I tried telling him, but that didn't work for him. I
don't think he valued my opinion because he didn't respect me.
So, how could he value what I had to say? I think you need to
understand something about me when it comes to relationships,
as well. For years friends have asked me how I could have stayed

faithful to Jackson when he was so far away. They have told me that they would have done the same thing that Jackson did. Physical needs are physical needs, and when two people are thousands of miles from one another, what do you do with that when you desire the physical closeness of another human being? And believe me, during that time, I had friends who offered to fill in for Jackson, if I needed. Men. When I say that I love someone, I mean physically as well as spiritually, I am theirs. I never doubted for a moment that I loved Jackson, or that his being so far away was any easier a time for him than I was having, but I promised him my love, physically as well as emotionally. Maybe it's because I'm, as my friend Luc says, an Aquarian. Years can go by, but I'll be there waiting, as I said I would. I have three sisters, but it took their gay brother to show them the meaning of fidelity. All three of them have been married multiple times and I swear they never left one husband that another man wasn't waiting in the wings as a safety net. That thing called fidelity. That's an Aquarian trait. That's us. We'll be there. You're in good hands with Allstate, or an Aquarian. I guess that he couldn't believe in that. He couldn't trust that I meant it when I told him I would wait for him. I get that from my mother. She was in love with my father from the moment they met. There was no other man for her. I can remember my parents being in love. I had seen it growing up. It was a wonderful thing to see. I believe that they took it for granted though, presuming that it would always be there. One day, my father strayed. He had an affair with a younger woman, someone we knew. I saw the regret in his face many years after it had happened. He went that one extra step when he shouldn't have and it destroyed his life. There was no way to undo what he had done. It destroyed my mom's life, as well. She existed after he left. But, she never loved another man, always my father, until she died. And the same for him regarding his feelings for her. But, he realized the depth of his love for my mother when it was too late. I swore I would never do that. The unhappiness it created between them that pervaded the rest of our years growing up was at times unbearable. You could feel it in the air. I especially dreaded the holidays. My mother would sit there, staring into space, lost somewhere in the past when times were better. So, when Jackson had his first affair, I called my mother and told her I knew how it felt and I wanted to know what to do. She told me, "If you love him, you have to forgive him. Do you want to stay with him? Then, let go of it and move beyond it, J. Or, leave now and never look back." I chose to stay. I don't know what made him do it; he didn't know what made him do it. Again, right from the very beginning, I tried talking with him about it. Jackson cannot bear to know he has made someone unhappy. He will do anything, anything, not to have to look into your eyes and see disappointment or emotional pain that he has caused. He will run so fast, it will stun you. So, I forgave him. How did I know he'd had an affair? That's in Chapter Three, under J.F. Oh, that one was an all-star, I'll tell ya, until he met me. But yes, I forgave Jackson and started from scratch. Remember, at the time he wasn't this big-shot vice-president of a company. He had just gotten off of supervising an assembly line in the plant, a Team Leader and had been made a line supervisor. He was starting in management. I just knew that boy was going places. Oh well, back to the messy part.

You could not get him to talk, though. I always felt that he was so used to being an executive and thinking like one that he forgot when he came home that there, he was just Jackson. He wasn't shooting off directives with me. I knew him when...and you can fill in that slot as you please, but that's how far back we went. We were in trouble and we both knew it and I wanted to talk about that. I'm a talker. I am an Aquarian. I like to talk things out. Jackson is a Leo. Forget about talking with a Leo. You just listen and then do. I had tried talking with Jackson when he came home for Christmas and we ended up in an argument because he kept walking away, finally telling me that if this kept up, if I kept insisting on talking, he probably wouldn't be here next Christmas. Fool that I was I thought he meant that he'd be spending it in Europe. Never did I think he meant as in, "Without you in my life." We had been through so much together; it never occurred to me that we wouldn't weather whatever had come between us. What I didn't know was that Jackson had had another affair. As was his habit, it turned out to be someone with whom he worked. An associate. Again. I kept asking him about it. I knew. I could tell from his behavior. How often does your lover come home and refuse to have sex with you? After 3+ months of being apart? Don't think so. As was his habit, he refused to discuss it with me. When that happened at Christmas, I was afraid to have sex with him at all and it was that Christmas that I took over another bedroom as my own. I realized that if he couldn't be open with me as in the past that I couldn't jeopardize my health any more than it had been. Terminally ill is terminally ill. You have just so many good days ahead of you and I wasn't about to cut those short because of Jackson's pride. So, since he wouldn't talk with me about it, I settled for option B, and moved into another bedroom. That may have been a mistake, but I was no longer in a frame of mind to deal with Jackson's ego and the pampering he felt he needed. The year before my mother had died in my arms and the anniversary of that had just passed. Plus the fact that I was supposedly dying, myself. Plus my back. A lot to deal with here, Jackson. Care to turn the page and get off of the subject of YOU for a moment? Guess not. That was my fault. There was never an issue at which time I forced Jackson to deal with it, because his career came first, therefore meaning that he always came first. Whatever emergencies there were, I dealt with them. I did the same when it came to my mother's illness and death, and when it came to my own health. He never had to worry about any of it. I made sure of that. Anyway...

Jackson had one more trip to the states while we were together; that was in either March or April of 1999, to prepare for moving to Charleston after accepting the position of vice-president. The plan as I knew it was that I was taking care of things in Massachusetts; the house, me, his daughter while she was there and going to school, etc. Our plan was to prepare the house to be sold, move to Charleston, open an antiques business and that way sell off all of the extra pieces that we had accumulated while living in the north. There was definitely a buyer's market in the south for northern antiques. We had discovered that on our trip to Macon a couple of years earlier when we went to Jackson's sister's house for Thanksgiving. So, we realized that we were on the right track and there wouldn't be much loss once we opened the shop. Plus, I had made enough connections in Massachusetts and the Rochester area in my dealings with other dealers to provide more pieces if we should be lucky at this and decide to keep the shop going. The network had been built. I was destroying my spine by painting all 13 rooms in the house, stripping wallpaper, painting trim in every room and hallway, etc. It actually came out rather well. I decided that the easiest thing to do was to paint everything that I could a uniform color. I chose a pale butter for the walls and bright white semi-gloss for all of the trim. And that was how I spent the last probably 15 months that we were in Massachusetts; tearing rooms apart, one by one, stripping wallpaper and re-plastering if it needed it, then good old-fashioned back-breaking painting; two dressing rooms, four bathrooms, all the trim work, two studies with fireplaces, six bedrooms, a kitchen, a butler's pantry and small side room, a dining room, two stairways and entry halls, and let's not forget about the living room the size of a football field complete with fireplace and bookshelves. Plus all of the ceilings. That was the hard part. All those damn ceilings. Thought my neck would never go back into place. In between of course, there was the landscaping to do, plus the memorial garden I had put in, in my mother's memory. There were the pets to take care of, which consisted of at one point in total and all at the same time mind you; two dogs, three cats, three fish tanks, eight pair of finches, and two budgies. In between all of this, I had trips to the hospital because of my back (No shit, Sherlock), requiring bed rest and three-four days of injections of Demerol until I could walk again. The best story that displays my own stupidity was the second-to-last Christmas that Jackson and his daughter spent at the house in Massachusetts. Here's an aside that you might enjoy. Christ, it can't all be pissing and moaning.

I "found" this huge, and I mean HUGE, Christmas tree. THE mother of all Christmas trees if there ever was one. It seemed larger than the one in the town square, I swear, and I only bought it because of the size of our living room. I knew that it would accommodate a tree that size without any problem. The living room was something like 18' x 28'. When empty, it looked like a football field. And, I wanted one Christmas that would be remembered above all the rest. The tree was something like 10' tall and 7' wide. I told you, it was a monster. But, beautiful. Not a bare spot to be seen. Perfect. Well, they delivered this thing and left it outside. My neighbor Chappie and I dragged the poor thing into the house, cut it down about a foot, and got it set up. I shut myself up in the house for three days, decorating the sucker. It took 4000+ lights alone to cover that baby. I had a friggin' ball. I was a kid again. Now I know why my father loved Christmas. I knew how he felt. It was the sort of tree that you threw boxes of ornaments on it and the tree devoured them. I broke the bank that year on decorating that tree, but it was worth every damn dime. Now, I would not let a soul into the house while I was decorating it and I kept the drapes on the front windows where we always put the tree, closed. No one could see it. Finally, when I finished and it passed the final rehearsal, I called Chappie and had him come over. "Holy Mother. Look at that friggin' tree..." I knew that if Chappie was impressed, it was a beautiful tree. Well, he brought over his wife, Annie, and I had her stand in the entryway of the living room with Chappie with her eyes closed and I plugged in the lights and...wham!! The living room was as bright as City Hall. She flipped. She had to sit down in the living room, alone, and stare at the tree. Then, she cried. She thought it was that beautiful. I have to admit, when I think back, it was overwhelming to see that tree. Of course nothing would satisfy Chappie, but to drag in the neighbors. And of course, I had to keep the drapes open so people could see it as they drove by, once they'd heard about it. It was too funny, really. My moment came when Jackson came home. I closed the drapes and unplugged the tree lights until he came in. I wouldn't let him go into the living room. So, he went upstairs and I asked him to come down the front stairway when I called him. As he did, I plugged in the lights. Like Annie, I cried. I saw in his eyes, the child he had been as he stared in awe at our Christmas tree. He stood there, with his mouth open, staring at our tree which was all alit with white lights and decorated in red bows, and white, red and clear ornaments from stem to stern and dusted off with tons of tinsel. It was breathtaking. Of course, the next big thrill was when his daughter arrived and saw the tree. Blew her right out of the water. It was probably the best Christmas the three of us had together. It's definitely the one I'll always remember. I had developed a sort of tradition for the three of us. I always wanted Christmas to be special because it meant that we would all be together as a family, and Jackson and his daughter came so far to do this and everyone worked so hard the rest of the year, looking ahead to when we would be together, that I decided one year to do a Christmas for the two of them about the 12 days of Christmas. So, I thought and thought about buying presents that maybe represented the 12 days, or a meal that represented the 12 days; nothing seemed to work. Finally, I decided that I would buy each of them 12 Christmas presents and that for the 11 days before Christmas, they would each open a present, but it had to be the present that I chose to be opened. The point being that I had wrapped them all and knew which presents were the important ones. Well, it worked. They loved it. Christmas always drove Jackson crazy because he couldn't stand knowing that there were presents hidden all over the house that he couldn't open. So, his daughter and I would have to chase him around or search him out, knowing that he was somewhere digging, looking for hidden presents. The idea stuck and got so bad that I would buy presents throughout the year and hide them all over the house so Jackson couldn't dig them out when he came home for Christmas and unwrap/re-wrap them so he'd know what he was getting for Christmas. He was a devil that way and an expert at unwrapping/re-wrapping presents. So, we had this huge tree and a great Christmas. Well, guess what? The night before Jackson was to go back to Europe and his daughter to go back to Georgia, my back exploded and I ended up in the hospital (Yet again) on Demerol. But, I at least had Christmas with them, and she came to see me before she left. Okay, scan ahead four days and the ambulance drops me off at the back door, okay? I walk in, stand there and take it all in because I loved coming home to our house, and headed into the living room. There stood the tree. Still standing there, still decorated with every light, every ornament, and every strand of tinsel. That's when MY jaw dropped and I got to stand in wonderment. Wondering how the hell I was going to take care of THIS problem without ending up right back in the hospital. So, I went into the garage, got a ladder and hauled it into the house and started taking off all of the lights and tinsel, ornaments and bows, boxed everything up and hauled it all to the attic, went back down and called Chappie to come over and bring his chain saw and the both of us stood there in the living room cutting the tree into parts so that we could get it out the front door. Merry Christmas, J. It was worth it, though. Had it been up to me, it would have stayed there, all decorated, in the living room windows forever. I just loved that tree. Best damn Christmas I've ever had and well worth the Demerol.

But, I digress...back to the pissing and moaning part.

In the midst of the painting and the pain, one Friday night about midnight, the phone rang. I remember it as being around the time that President Clinton was possibly going to be impeached. The Monica and blue-dress thing. Why? Probably because of all of Jackson's philandering, I suppose. I sort of felt that I knew what Hillary was going through and admired her for her strength because she was always looking at the bigger picture, whereas Bill settled for whatever seemed to drop into his lap, pardon the pun. So, the phone rings and I was in bed, reading. It was Jackson. Right off the bat, I knew something was wrong. Jackson was predictable. The phone call always came on Saturday afternoon, like clockwork. Here he was calling me late on a Friday night. Hmm...what was wrong with this picture? He called to tell me that he'd accepted the position in Charleston and that he'd be going back to Brussels to close up the apartment there and bring back his things...to Charleston. Directly to Charleston?? Yes, directly to Charleston, no stopping in Massachusetts. There IS something wrong with this picture. So, I finally had to ask him what was wrong. At first he denied that anything was wrong. He told me that it wasn't something he could discuss over the phone. I finally reminded him that I knew him well and I knew that something was on his mind; something was wrong, and I wanted him to tell me about it now, instead of my having to wait until he returned from Europe and somehow made time to come to the house. Tell me now, Jackson. I don't think I'll ever forget what he said next. It was so simple and to the point..."I'm coming to Charleston. You're not." I am so stupid when I shouldn't be. I presumed he meant that I wasn't coming to Charleston right then and there, that I'd have to stay in Massachusetts until the house was put on the market and sold, etc. So, I'm going, "Oh, I wasn't planning on coming down until everything here was settled, anyway." "No, J. You're not listening to what I'm saying. **I'm** moving to Charleston. You're **NOT** moving to Charleston. We're through, breaking up. This is done." I remember repeating several times, "What is it you're saying, Jackson?" It would not register with me. I felt we'd made it this far, we had some trouble and needed to talk things out, but break up? That had not yet crossed my mind. I could tell by the tone in his voice that for him it was already a given. For him, it was a done deal. At some point, I could hear his voice but not register what he was saying to me and finally I told him that I couldn't listen to any more and had to hang up. Sleep? What was that? Not that night, or for a few more to come soon after, like 1000. I looked out into the hallway at the ladder and paint cans and started let out this blood-curdling scream. I knew that this time it was for real. He was through. I knew him that well. I got up and started pacing through the entire house, from room to room, over and over, crying and hyperventilating. Calling out to my mother, God, whomever. Didn't matter. "This is done." At about 4:30 a.m., I finally stopped crying enough so that I could lie down on the bed. There was no one to call. My mother was dead. My family wasn't speaking to me. I couldn't call Jackson and tell him the bad news, now could I? What to do..??? If I could just stop pacing and get my heart out of my mouth and back into my chest where it belonged. Many of you will understand this feeling. You know the one you get in the middle of the night in the pit of your stomach that wakes you out of a sound sleep? That ache that you think will never go away? Like you're free-falling and can't grab onto anything as you're spiraling down and down...For months I would wake up out of a dead sleep, night after night with that scared feeling and that ache in the pit of my gut. Scared of what?? I was never quite sure, but I sure was scared when I woke up. Or, the nights when I actually did finally fall asleep, only to dream of Jackson and jump up in bed, thinking he was there and realizing that I was all alone. I am going to tell you that there are far worse things in life than dying. Try a sleepless night with a broken heart every night for say three years. I think it was a year before I actually stopped bursting into tears unexpectedly; anywhere, at any given time. Restaurants, church, the grocery store, in bed, in the shower, visiting friends, in the car. No place was safe for me or from me. No place offered peace and comfort. That place was Charleston and I wasn't going. "This is done."

At about 7:00 a.m. the phone rang. Of course I was up. Wasn't everybody? Hadn't they heard yet? I presumed it was Jackson calling back, wanting to explain. No. It was Nelson, the psychic in Rochester. He had just come back home from the Cleveland Clinic. He'd been very ill recently with a lung ailment and had been sent from Rochester to Cleveland for treatment. On his return, he said that he had to call me because I had been on his mind for several days and he needed to talk with me immediately. He needed to talk with me?? I was speechless. I couldn't believe it. How bizarre is that?? Naturally, I broke down. I started blubbering like a fool, and he told me that he wanted me to try and calm down, that he had something important to tell me and I needed to listen to him because it would help me later on. God bless you, Nelson, wherever you are my friend. You saved my life that morning. What Nelson told me basically was what had just taken place in my conversation with Jackson. He reminded me that he had told me several times that Jackson would leave me, but I wouldn't believe Nelson. That's true, I wouldn't. I believed that he was wrong. He wasn't. He told me that I would see Jackson again, face to face, and that Jackson would find that upsetting because he didn't want to face me. To him, it was already over and he wanted to move on with his life. However, I would see him again and that I would have my say when I did. He told me that Jackson would go from one relationship to another and look for what he had with me, but never find it. That he would always know where I was and how I was doing and that the day would come when my fortunes would rise and his would fall, and that the day would also come when I would realize that I had moved beyond my love for Jackson and I would meet someone and that relationship would last the rest of my life, but that Jackson would look and never find what we had and would come to regret what he had done, but realize that it was too late, that I had moved beyond him. He told me that I felt very confused and afraid, that I felt everything had been taken from me, but to give it time and be patient, mine would come to me. This was a learning experience and I had to be aware of that and glean from it what I could so I would know better next time. As Nelson put it, "You have to stay the course, J., and you'll be all right. I can see it." What a shame I couldn't. I do now, though. But then, it was all one miserable, scary mess that I was facing alone. Oddly enough, that was the last reading Nelson ever did for me, but he made sure that I got that message and I have played that over and over in my mind many times to try and calm me so that I could focus. And, he was right. As of this writing, Jackson is on his fourth relationship since we broke up six years ago. I've yet to start my first. Thank you again, Nelson. May God bless you.

Chapter Fifteen

"What Now, My Love?"

Naturally, I said my Rosary. Hey, I'm Italian AND Catholic. What else do we do? Other than wear black forever after our spouses die, and that only seems to be okay for Italian women. I've never known an Italian man to do that. Anyway, I said my Rosary, and I said my Rosary every day for about 2 years after that. It allowed me to focus. It calmed me, which was exactly what I needed. I went to church every morning. That helped calm me. And, what would I have done without my friends? Oh, my God, what would I have done without them? They were all angels, all put in place at a time when I desperately needed them. What they didn't tolerate from me during that year that I spent in Massachusetts. They were incredible. Patient, understanding, kind, giving, never did any of them ever tell me to shut up or to just get on with it...never. They let me be me, whatever form that took, and they were always there. To all of you, my love and gratitude. Physically, I had no idea what was going on. I'm sure that alarms were going off all over the place inside, but I didn't have time for it right at that moment. I'm sure my liver was doing a dance and my back, but hey. There were things to do. First of all, about three days after Jackson's phone call, I woke up to the sound of hammering. When I looked out the window, a real estate agent was banging a "For Sale" sign into the ground. "Hello." Yep, the bastard put it up for sale the following Monday. He wasn't going to waste any time, was he? He called me that night, the sweet soul. "Thanks for the warning, Jackson," I said. "J., I'm working and I don't have the time to deal with all of this. I told you we were through. Did you think I was actually going to move to Charleston and keep the house in Massachusetts??" "Not exactly, but I didn't think or know that things were going to start happening right now. Where do you expect me to go, Jackson? You told me where I'm not going. But, where am I supposed to go?" As with everything else, Jackson already had a plan in mind. "I want you to bring the real estate papers to Charleston." Personally, I have always believed that Jackson wanted me near so I wouldn't destroy anything in the house or burn it down, altogether. I'd learned that his ex-wife was that type, but I wasn't. When he told her that they were through, she clobbered him over the head with a rather large bottle of Clinique and sat on him and beat the crap out of him. Can't say as I would blame her.

Okay, so I pack a bag and to Charleston I go. I don't remember the drive to Boston or the trip to Charleston. None of it. Just that I went. Somehow, Jackson found the time to pick me up at the airport. He was not happy. I was. I was away from that house and all it represented. He was his usual cold, stoic self when he wasn't getting his way. So, I finally asked what the matter was and he said, "I didn't want you to come here, but I had no choice. Now, you're NOT staying. You're going back at the end of the week." I'm not staying? Whose idea was this?? "I need to sign off on the papers you brought and I am picking up a new car this weekend. That's why you are here, to help me." Oh.is.that.so?? I looked at him, probably seeing the "real" him for the first time in the ten years we had been together, and said, "I want you for once to have the balls to tell me to my face that we're through, Jackson. You've never had the courage in the past to tell me anything to my face. Now, you're going to do it. And that is why I am here. Not for your stupid real estate papers and definitely not to help you start your new life without me. You took that step long before you ever decided to tell me anything. Just once, I want to hear you say the words while you are actually with me, face to face buddy, instead of you having the built-in security of being miles away from me so you don't have to deal with the mess you created." He was furious, but I would not budge. For one solid week I waited and waited. I would sit in that apartment of his and when he was there, I would stare at him. His sister had called and thought it a good idea if we all went to Savannah for a break. What an idiot. As if this had been some sort of disagreement we were having. What can I tell you; Southerners with their air of denial. Jackson agreed. Anything, I think, not to have to come home to my constant staring and waiting for an explanation.

First however, we stopped to pick up his new SUV, and drove his rental back to the agency. Then, to Savannah. It was a very quiet drive for the two of us. Jackson wanted to talk about everything as if it was all over and done with, as if we were somehow over all of this and still friends and communicating with one another. This was a bump in the road and I needed to make it an easy adjustment for him, as I had always done before. Didn't I realize the pressure he was under at his new job? How could I want to go on discussing something that was upsetting to him and in the past? And this is what I listened to when he finally decided to "open up" during our drive that day. He seemed to forget that his past was sitting next to him in his new SUV. Finally, he put on a CD and said, "I have something I want you to listen to. It will explain everything." I hear Bocelli's "Time to Say Goodbye." I hit the eject button, yanked out that poor CD and whipped it into the back of the SUV. "You fucking coward... The best you can do at a moment when you should be expressing your own feelings is to throw on a fucking CD and expect that to satisfy me?? You expect that to answer my questions and for me to forgive you?? As far as I'm concerned, you're a lying, cheating prick of a coward, Jackson! You have no soul! You have no morals! You are trash! No matter how you pretty it up, or how successful you become, you're still a pile of shit. I have wiped better than you from my ass! Now, if you want to turn this car around and head back to Charleston, go right ahead! I have nothing more to say to you and I can see Savannah on my own, when I want! I do not need you or your family to do it as some sort of consolation prize..."

And that took care of any further conversation between us. I actually felt 100% better after tearing him apart and went on to have a great time in Savannah. He sort of tagged along behind us, marking time. The night before we left Savannah, Jackson's sister decided to let me know that she was aware for months that there were problems between us, that Jackson had spoken to her quite often about the situation. Oh, really? So, I turned on her, reminding her that I was the one who helped bring them back together as a family after years of not speaking with one another, and that this is how she decided to repay my kindness? I said, "Fuck you." The end of that relationship. No great loss in my book. And believe me, the drive back the following morning was without conversation AND without any CD being played.

Arriving back in Charleston, his daughter called that night and wanted to talk with me. She told me that she was coming to North Carolina that week for Spring break and wanted to see me before I left. I told her that I'd love to see her, but it was her father's decision to make, not mine. I wanted him to be the one to say "No" to her about this, something she found important. The refusal was not going to come from me. He told her no, that I had to go back before she arrived. It was easy to see that Jackson had already begun the process of cutting me entirely out of his life. My confusion over this came from the fact that I really had not given him any problem about it and except for the "Savannah" incident, had gone along with everything he had said. He wanted me gone.

I awoke the next morning to have Jackson tell me that I was leaving...that morning. "Go pack, J. I've made the arrangements. You're flight is this afternoon." So, that afternoon, he left work early, picked me up and we went to the airport. Now, here's the stupid part. I wanted him to drop me at the curb, but he insisted on coming in, probably to make sure that I actually got on the damn plane and left. He walked me to security, I handed them my carry-on and turned around to say goodbye and there stood Jackson, as he had on so many occasions in the past, balling like a baby. "This is your idea Jackson, not mine. This is what you want, but you're the one crying. Goodbye, Jackson." I walked through security, picked up my bag and never looked back.

Time to take a break. I've gotten too close to this, again...Okay, I'm better now. Went out onto the deck and had a smoke...or 12.

I started with the books that I'd collected over the years. I love books. Love to read. Takes me to another world. I had books in every room of the house. At the end of the count, I had hauled 38 boxes of books, CD's, record albums, and VHS tapes to the local library for their spring book sale. They were real happy. I began separating everything; I only wanted the things that I bought and/or what I could actually use and figured I'd be in a one-bedroom apartment or studio for the time being, so I had to "scale down." Tons of plastic garbage bags loaded with clothes, drapes, towels and linens went to the Salvation Army. I called everyone and told them to come over and take whatever they wanted. Less for me to pack. I knew what Jackson wanted to keep (He'd given me a list) and that had all been set aside and packed (By me). I had pulled my belongings and furniture out and what was left was given away. My friends had a field day. Swedish bowls that cost $1000 each were handed over. "Take it. I don't want it. Just another memory." I was serious. Most of the "gifts" over the years from Jackson were because he'd had another affair. As the years went by, the gifts became more expensive and I began to dread seeing a package in his hands when he came home. Bad karma. I wanted nothing to do with them. This was his gilt-edged guilt. I wasn't about to carry that shit around with me. They all came with his tears and I never found any joy in any of those gifts. He was the one who needed to show people how successful he was, not me. Take 'em.

Jackson came back to Massachusetts to sign off on the final papers, meet the new owners, and to show the movers what to take. He also had to sign the lease on my new apartment. Sorry, but being on Social Security, no money in the bank thanks to Jackson, I had nowhere to go. So, I called him and told him that either he signed the lease on an apartment for a year or I was going to take him to court and sue him for palimony. Massachusetts recognizes same-sex relationships and we had been together for over ten years. When we came back from signing the lease for the apartment, there was nothing left to do. I had gone up to my room and was lying on my bed trying to convince myself that this was really happening, that the time had come to say goodbye. Until we went to the apartment, Jackson had busied himself with the new owners, the movers, and had basically ignored me. I had no idea what he had in mind, probably just to leave. Not wanting to see that, I went and stayed in my room, lying there, staring at the ceiling. Shortly after that, I heard him coming up the back stairway and walking into my room. He came over and sat on the edge of the bed. I remember him putting his hand on my shoulder and saying, "I want to talk with you before I leave. I know that this hasn't been easy for you and I've tried to do everything to make sure you'll be all right." At that, I remember him coming around to the other side of the bed and lying down next to me and putting his arms around me. I lay there thinking, "I have to remember what this feels like because it's going to be the last time he ever holds me." And so, I let him hold me while I cried. It reminded me of the beginning of our relationship, when he first went to Europe. Talk about coming full circle. He asked if we could make love. Believe me, as much as I may have wanted to feel that closeness with him again, it was too much to ask at that particular time. I jumped up out of the bed. Bad back or not, I was not going to be totally destroyed when he walked out of that house. So I told him, "Jackson, there's no point to that now. It would only hurt. Don't do this to me," and I went downstairs to the kitchen and stood at the kitchen sink, crying. He came down after me and stood at the counter, trying to explain, and he broke down. I remember going over to him and putting my hand on his face and saying to him, "Please Jackson, tell me why any of this happened. I need to know why." I never should have asked. St. Theresa said, "More tears have been shed over answered prayers than unanswered prayers."

He told me that his leaving me had nothing to do with how much he loved me. He raised his arms, sort of out of frustration, and crossed the kitchen before he continued. With his head down, staring at the kitchen floor, he finally said, "I tried doing the right thing. I tried doing what my father had done for my mother. I tried staying because you're ill, but...you didn't die. **You were supposed to die.** I can't go into this new job and the pressures involved and keep wondering when the phone call will come, when the doctors will finally be right. When I came home after you hemorrhaged, I didn't expect to find you here AND healthy. When you opened the door, I realized that this had to come to an end because I couldn't take the stress of it any more. If you were to come to Charleston with me and my job should ever discover you, I'd be through. They'd never keep me. I've worked too hard and come too far to jeopardize all of that. I can't risk it and I can't take the stress of you and the job. One of you has to go. Maybe in the future, when things are more secure for me at work, if your health holds out, maybe then we can get back together. Maybe then it will work again. I don't know. For right now, it has to stop. I have to leave you here." Have you ever been punched in the stomach, in the solar plexus? It leaves you with this radiating ache that spreads out from your abdomen like ripples on a pond and knocks the wind right out of your sails. I couldn't believe what I was hearing. I remember having my hands wrapped around my stomach and my mouth opening to speak, but nothing would come out. I don't even know if I was breathing. All I could hear was the sound of my heart beating over the sound of his voice and I wanted him to stop. I didn't want to hear this. I didn't want to know this. How the hell do you deal with that sort of information, with that sort of cold, calculated reasoning? "You didn't die." Let me tell you that I have wandered through life for years with that phrase running through my mind. There is nothing in life that holds any value after someone you love tells you something that crippling to your entire being. If this is how someone who loves me feels, what the hell can I expect from life? What scared me most was that I could love someone for almost 11 years and not have seen this side of them.

For the first time in my life, I didn't rationalize the situation. I couldn't, it was that overpowering. Son-of-a-bitch. Can you beat that? I didn't die. This is why I tell people that I forgave Jackson long ago for leaving, but I doubt I'll ever get beyond how he did it. I'd rather he had lied to me.

I went into the living room and sat on one of my boxes and I realized that for all these years I had it wrong. It had all been a lie. Here I was, fighting to stay alive for my mother and Jackson; fighting doctors, my family, my friends, even my lover, not knowing that at some point he had turned a corner and was just waiting for me to die so he could get on with his own life. That's when reality settled in and I let go and cried until I sat there, heaving and couldn't cry anymore. When all else fails, sit your ass down and have yourself a damn good cry. As my mother used to say, "It cleanses the soul."

There is something about an intense relationship, the type where the couple shares the most extraordinary things, that it seers you to one another emotionally. Someone explained to me once that what Jackson and I had went beyond any ordinary relationship; it went beyond the bounds of a marriage. Because of the emotional intensity involved, what with my being ill and my mother's illness and death, and our being separated for so long, it's like fighting a war together. You watch out for each other's backs, always keeping an eye open monitoring everything. You will never experience that type of "fox-hole buddy" relationship again because the circumstances are so unique and you tell one another things that you wouldn't even tell your wives or parents. Out of necessity that level of intimacy is forced upon the two of you. My friend explained to me that this is what Jackson and I had, and when it ends, there is nothing else in life to compare it with. It's as if you've lost your other half and are no longer whole.

Chapter Sixteen

"Time to Say Goodbye..."

M y feelings on why he left? After all these years, I've come to believe the above paragraphs are the truth. I believe it because I know Jackson. I know how weak a person he is. His strength is in the world of corporate business. He thrives on that game. He's a Leo and that's his jungle, his domain. I'm an Aquarian. My strength is in my personal life. I believe that a job is eight hours out of your day. Punch in, give it your best, and leave. Then get on with the important things in your life. I also know that I became Jackson's conscience. His moral indicator. I tell people that our relationship was like Wilde's, "The Portrait of Dorian Gray." Jackson had all the fun and I had the scars to prove it. To do what he did in the way that he did it, he had to leave town. The perfect getaway. He didn't have to stick around and see the mess he'd created; he didn't have to view the disappointment. He didn't have to see the heartache. Remember, I'm the one who always cleaned up the messes. And brother, this was one hell of a mess.

It's funny how little things come back to you after a time; as if your mind can't absorb the shock of it all when it first happens and lets bits and pieces in after a while. And everything you hear about a breakup is true. The magnitude of it is incredible. I had never realized that so much of my life revolved around Jackson until he left. It was over a year before I slept through an entire night. Waking up in a sweat, dreaming about him, and realizing that he wasn't there, that it was real. That is the worst feeling. I used to hate that, just dreaded going to bed. So, I'd stay up until I was half dead and crawl to bed. Sure enough, about three hours later, there I was bolt upright in the damn bed. Another dream. The most crushing feeling of all was knowing that the person who was your life had gotten on with theirs and was thriving. I can't tell you how many hours I spent wondering how awful it must have been for Jackson being with me, that he could go to Charleston and actually live his life with such immediacy. At first, I never heard from him. Then, he started calling. The thrill of that first phone call was amazing to me. I felt alive again. As usual though, it was all about him; how tired he was, how stressed he was with work, the incredible responsibilities he carried. This went on for several weeks. Like clockwork, like when we were together; every Saturday there was his phone call. Finally, I got up the nerve to tell him that I really wasn't interested in hearing how awful his life was. I told him that we were no longer a couple and that now I didn't have to listen to his fears and worries, that was no longer my responsibility, and I could tell that he hadn't found anyone yet to be with, or he wouldn't be calling me. That took care of the phone calls. One day, I was talking with Jackson's daughter on the phone. Yes, his daughter. She was one of my anchors after her father left. I told you, a wonderful girl. As we were talking, she made a comment about how stressful she found my relationship with her father toward the end and was glad that it was over. I asked her to back up for a moment and explain. As far as I knew, she knew very little about the problems in our relationship, at least from my side of the fence, until after we broke up. She proceeded to tell me that her father had called her before he came back from Europe and asked her to spy on me for him. Spy on me?? Yes, spy on me. I can only guess that he was looking for something to bolster his reasons for leaving, but he found nothing. Who was I having the affair with, in Gardner, the damn mailman?? I was reminded of something my mother used to say, "A man will always accuse you of what he is actually doing himself." How true. Apparently, before Jackson would call me on Saturday, he would call his daughter at her boyfriend's house and ask her if anything had happened during the week that he should know about before calling me. She said that she would tell him that there was nothing to tell him, but he would keep calling. I asked her why she didn't tell him to do his own dirty work. She told me something that then made sense out of Jackson's relationships with everyone in his family. She said, "He signs the checks." After our phone call, I sat in my living room and pondered that one for a while. It was true. There was no one that I could think of who would mention anything emotional about Jackson; no one person told me that they missed his sense of humor, what a kind person he had been, or the way he could make them laugh if they were down about something. No one. They all mentioned the money. I took a long, hard look at myself at that point and I realized something very important that I would never forget. Wherever I have gone, however long I have been away or talked with someone, they always, always mention how much they've missed me, missed having me around, missed our conversations, and missed the laughter. I have a friend in Gardner, Alan, a wonderful guy. He saw me through a lot of this. I talked with him about two weeks ago and he said to me, "You have no idea how much I miss having you here. I miss our conversations. No one makes me laugh the way you do." I also realized that both of Jackson's former secretaries, Nancy and Carole, kept in touch with me, not with Jackson. Now, what the hell does that tell you? Carole is an angel. She sends me Christmas cards, we e-mail one another. Whenever she travels, I get the most beautiful postcards and notes from her. When the doctors told me that I was going to live, Carole was the first person I called. I told her, this was more important than an e-mail. She had been through everything with me, right from the beginning. I had to call her to tell her the good news. Actually, she had just gotten out of the shower when her husband told her I was on the phone. I never call Carole, so she was concerned. I had to tell her, personally, and thank her for her YEARS of prayers. Another incredible person that God put into my life.

That one phone call with his daughter, that one comment that she made, started turning my life around. "He signs the checks." I realized that it didn't matter what I had or who I was, I had people in this world that cared about me, as a person. I was surrounded by people who cared about what happened to me, as a person. They didn't care about my checkbook, or how I could help them. They cared about me. It occurred to me that Jackson was surrounded by people who only valued him for what he could do for them. I had one more phone call from his daughter. Again, she was upset about something her father had said or done. I realized that this couldn't go on. I needed to distance myself from Jackson and his life, and start rebuilding mine. So, I listened to her and tried to calm her down, and I told her that I needed to tell her something and I hoped that she would understand. I needed to distance myself from her and her father, and try to get on with my life. I told her that I couldn't do that while I still had connections to him. I needed to begin the process of putting Jackson in the past and that I found dealing with him and his family didn't allow that process to begin. I told her that I loved her and didn't want this to hurt her, but that I needed to "hunker down" for a while, let the dust settle and the give the wounds some time to begin healing. I stressed to her that this wasn't a loss, that I would come back into her life if she would let me, at some point, but right now I needed to heal and talking about her father and trying to help her deal with and understand his actions and reasons for doing things wasn't helping me because it kept me there, in the past. All of them had to learn how to deal with him now. The years that I put in acting as a buffer between Jackson and his family and his life, were over. That poor girl. She said that she understood and told me to please get in touch with her when I felt that I could. I felt that I had to take that action. I could feel myself sinking, between talking with his daughter and talking with Jackson, I was spinning my wheels in shit. He was still getting the benefits of our relationship together, only without my being there. He still had someone to vent all of his frustrations on, but I was left in Gardner to try and figure out how to rebuild my own life. This was NOT how it was supposed to go. I then took a serious look at my own life, what there was of it, and decided that I really wanted to go back to school and try and finish my college degree. That has always been my dream, to get my degree. It has taken me the better part of my life to do this and I still haven't gotten there, but I will. You see, that was part of the "plan" that Jackson and I had. When he achieved his goal of vice-president, then it was supposed to be MY turn. Our plan was to move to Charleston. I was going to go back to school and finish my degree. Yea, a great plan. We all know what happened.

I had to also deal with my family. There were demons there that went back decades and it was time to clean house, altogether.

I was visiting with my family shortly after Jackson had left. It was for the holidays. Not a good time to be dealing with grief, death, betrayal, deceit, abandonment, etc., and having a family that felt you had let them down.

For some rare and unexplainable reason, the four of us were all sitting together at the table in my older sister's kitchen. It was the day after Christmas. My brother-in-law was standing at the kitchen sink. I remember this because when my older sister, his wife, made her comment to me, he dropped his cup in the sink. Sitting there, I was trying miserably to be a part of the here and now, when suddenly my older sister said to me, "You know, your being gay is what killed mom. It broke her heart." That immediately brought me into the here and now. I thought, "That's it. That is the last insult." I looked at my brother-in-law, who had dropped his cup and spun around to look at my sister, as if she were totally out of her mind, and I looked directly at my sisters, all sitting there, all judging me again like when we were kids. I looked back at my older sister and said slowly and deliberately so I wouldn't lose my temper, "It amazes me to sit and look at the three of you. Here, all my life, the three of you condemned me, always calling me 'queer' instead of by my name. I was never anything to any of you until you started having children. Suddenly you all realized that you had a built-in babysitter and then I had a name!" I pointed at my older sister. "And you, when you were pregnant with your first child. You had the gall when I asked you what you wanted, to say to me, 'Anything, as long as it isn't like you.' Well, well, well. Here we now sit together for the first time in years. And the one thought that comes to my mind is that of the four of us, I am the only one sitting at this table that has not stood before a judge. I am the only one of the four of us who has not spent time in jail. I am the only one WITHOUT a police record." Pointing at each sister, I said, "Drugs, alcohol, shoplifting." I got up and looking at my older sister, said, "I doubt very much if my being gay is what killed mom or broke her heart. We all share in that responsibility. And, remember one thing; I am the one she wanted to be with when she knew she was ill. It wasn't any of you that held her in your arms when she was dying, it was me. I was given that honor. I have no regrets when it comes to mom. I did everything that I could for her, including being there when she died so she wasn't alone in some nursing home. Where were all of you?" I stood up and I remember my brother-in-law looking at my older sister and saying, "You idiot. What is the matter with you?" As my sisters sat there, staring at one another, I looked at my brother-in-law and walked out the door. I have never been back. I told you, my sisters are like buried landmines. You never know when one will go off. You always have to be ready for an explosion of some kind; however, for once, I was the unexpected explosion.

So, I went back to Massachusetts and called the local community college and sent for an application. I spent two semesters taking courses and making Dean's List and Honor's List(Thank you) both semesters. I was damn proud of myself, too. During that time, I started looking around me and realized that I was living physically in the remnants of my relationship with Jackson. So, one day, I started packing things; presents from

Jackson, jewelry from Jackson, everything that I could find, and set the boxes in the closet. One thing that his daughter had asked me for was our love letters. She told me that she had never known an emotional side to her father and she would like to have them. The conversation came up one day because she had asked me if I still had mine and I told her that I had, but that her father had thrown my letters to him in the garbage when he moved out, and I found them while I was cleaning out the house, and kept them. Yea, a real romantic that guy. So, she asked me that if I ever got rid of them, would I send them to her and I told her that I would. So, they went to a new home, as well. It dawned on me that I was still wearing the ring he'd given me so many years before. I loved that ring and what it represented to me. One day, I took it off and put it away. Okay, so keeping everything in the closet to me was like hiding a body in there. It drove me nuts knowing those boxes were in that closet, because I was refusing to carry out the next step which for me was to send them back to him. That weekend, down to the post office I went with the boxes. I sent everything certified mail and insured to his office in Charleston. I put the ring in a separate box and wrote him a note. I told him that he wouldn't understand, but that I needed to get on with my own life now and that these things were constant reminders of what had been and I needed to get rid of them. I couldn't sell them or throw them away, so I left it up to him since they were presents from him, to do with as he wanted. No, it's bad Karma to sell or throw stuff away. They were presents from him, so to him they went. Their future was his choice, not mine. As was true with him, they had only been mine temporarily. I will admit though that when I returned his ring, I cried, because I knew then that I was beginning to really let go and accept what had happened. That ring was my symbol of "couple." No more, though. Well, it didn't take long for the phone to ring. "Yes Jackson, I know you're upset." "You're being spiteful and selfish." I'm being spiteful and selfish?? Right. "No Jackson, I'm trying to get on with my life without you. I told you that you wouldn't understand." "Well, are you any happier now that you've sent back the ring?" "Happier? No. Do I feel that I'm headed in that direction? Yes. This is the beginning, Jackson. Guess what? You can't do anything about it now. You relinquished that right, and I think that it's time to say goodbye, Jackson, for now anyway." He was not a happy camper with my decision. How could he be? He thought that he'd still have some sort of control over me, even now. Well, he did. But, I wasn't about to acknowledge it or let him know the truth. It was five years later that I realized he really wasn't coming back. FIVE YEARS... One day, sitting at home and I heard a song, the same damn song that he insisted I listen to, that Andrea Bocelli thing, "Time to Say Goodbye." And, it struck me that he really wasn't coming back, and what was so depressing was that I still had that thought somewhere buried in my mind and expected it to happen. Your own mind will set out land mines like this for you to trip over and set off. Why do we sabotage ourselves like this? So we will quit deluding ourselves and face the truth.

I had been accepted to a school in the state of Washington. A counselor at school had told me about a very interesting and different college that was outside of Olympia, WA, that I might like. So, I applied and was accepted. I found it intriguing because I felt that in my quest for a new life, this was one spot in the world where Jackson and I had no history, whatsoever. We'd been to California, lived all over the northeast, and had been to the south to visit his family and for vacations. Ah, but the northwest...never. Virgin territory. Time to make another life-altering decision. Do I put everything that was left in storage or trek it cross country? Well, since there was no money to be had for this trip, once again, I sold what I could and gave the rest away. No memories, no traces of a life in New England. Gone. All of it. I then focused on getting my car AND myself ready to travel across this great expanse called the USA, and all by myself. Not an easy task, when you're supposed to be terminally ill and have a crippling back disorder. But, I did it, and I thank God. For, in going to the northwest, I found doctors who would treat my deteriorating back problem with two surgeries in a month. I found a dental surgeon who extracted 11 teeth which had been destroyed because of all of the drugs I was taking. I also found a doctor who told me that I was actually killing myself with the type of pain killers I was taking which was part of the reason I had gained almost 70 pounds. Between that and the blockers I was on for my liver problem, I was one bloated mess of toxins and fluid. So, I decided to wean myself from all the drugs I was taking except for the medication to control the hepatitis virus. Between doing that, and the new pain killers I was prescribed, I lost 70 pounds in less than two months. I do NOT prescribe this as a form of treatment for anyone. I was at a point where I realized that I had to take control of my body, even if that meant dying in the process. I was tired of gaining weight and feeling so bloated all the time. I looked horrible. Well, it worked. And, I've never gained back any of the weight. Again, I have to say that it was trusting in my own instincts and listening to that little voice in the back of my head telling me that I could do this. What did I have to lose? According to the physicians, I should have already been dead. So, I went to the northwest with the dream of obtaining my college degree. I ended up however, earning much more.

Listen, when you've been hemorrhaging and racing in an ambulance to a hospital, you realize one very important thing. There isn't a damn thing you can do but go along for the ride. You realize that you are just a part of the process at that point, so you might as well relax. Getting upset isn't going to change anything. It is totally out of your control. Having experienced all that I have with my illness, I learned one very important thing. What is it that the Angels say when they appear in the Bible…"Be Not Afraid". What good does it do to fear the unknown? The odds are against you from the start, so you might as well remain calm and have a clear head. Your body is doing enough trying to monitor and maintain some sort of physical balance to get you through this emergency. Stress will only make it worse.

Chapter Seventeen

"Me and My Shadow"
"You're better than that. You're better than
you know" -
Norman to Esther, "A Star Is Born"

I want to know at the end of telling this story that I can see that I did love Jackson and that he loved me. I regret that he didn't love me enough at the end to be able to sit down and tell me we were through and explain it to me, instead of doing it the way he did. That left me with no dignity and a LOT of questions that went unanswered. It made me believe and see that there is only one real sin in this world, that of deliberate cruelty. I want to leave this knowing that I wouldn't have done the same thing to him because my understanding of loving someone really was different than his. That's what I want to take from this experience. That I tried to do the decent thing at all times with Jackson. That would help me move beyond this. Something about this episode in my life would not allow me to move on until I looked at it. I refused for years to do that. I would talk about different episodes if someone asked, or if something reminded me of an incident, funny or otherwise, but I would not stop long enough to look at the relationship en bloc. Because of that, I know that I have not been able to move on in my life. I know that

I was to learn something from this experience, but I didn't have the strength to turn around and look at the demons that I thought were chasing me. You see, for years I saw it as a failure of mine. It wasn't. So, I had to dig in my heels, turn around and look at this crazy thing in my life and give it the attention it needed in order to teach me what I needed to know.

And by doing that, it gave me the strength to look at ALL of the experiences in my life that then led me to accepting my relationship with Jackson as it was, rather than accepting that it was unhealthy, and leaving of my own choice.

If you don't build a life after something like this, then this becomes your life, and the pain of it becomes your emotional life. The one "truth" about life that Jackson taught me is that there is really only one mortal sin we carry and that is having the ability to inflict the act of deliberate cruelty upon another. That is to me the ultimate evil in life. Even harder when it comes from someone you love.

As for the positive's...looking back at this has made me realize that I was in love with Jackson, from the very beginning. I'd always refused to see that. That would have been too painful before. I have the ability to love and fall in love and now, I can do it again with the right person and for the right reason. That being? Because I deserve it. Just learning that was worth going back through it all over again.

I am a good person. I am a decent human being. I forgive myself for how I allowed (It is very important to acknowledge that **we allow** people to treat us as they do, and that **we allow** them into our lives) Jackson to treat me (Because I was in love with him). The realization of self.

According to my doctors, I am now going to live. After 11 years of fighting this insidious and unwelcome intruder into my life, I am finally winning the battle. After years of fighting doctors, family, my lover, all of whom believed that I was in denial and would not accept the fact that I was dying, I have lived long enough to prove all of them wrong. I have stood by and buried my parents, my stepfather, my niece, knowing that people there wondered why it wasn't me in that hole. I held my mother in my arms when she died, knowing that she saw my life as a failure and worried how I would survive without her. I watched my lover walk out the door, after telling me that he had stayed as long as he could, waiting for me to die, but I didn't. Is the taste of victory sweet? Let me say, it is just sweet enough to cover the bitter after-taste of life's disappointments. I had to go through all of it though to get where I am today. It was and is my life to care about and take responsibility for, no one else's.

Now, you can flip that coin and say that what Jackson failed to realize seven years ago was that by telling me the truth that last day we shared alone together, the two of us in that otherwise empty house, that I did die. I died that day when Jackson uttered those words that became my death sentence. Jackson knew what he was doing, knew what he was saying and the impact it would have. I even began to refer to myself as one of the "walking dead," and with good reason. Jackson not only broke my heart that day, he tried to make sure that there would be none left for a chance at revival, he tried breaking my spirit; however, once again, Jackson underestimated my ability to survive. It has taken me all these years to realize that it is all in how you perceive it to be. I refused to let that be the end of my life. I refused to become my mother, the victim. Instead, I recreated my self. And, when I no longer needed the vestiges of what Jackson left behind; my physical being, my name, my family, I divested myself of them. If Jackson had not opened my eyes to the lie I was living, I would have been content to stay there in my pain. I could have believed him and followed that path to my real death or, I could have moved back home with my family, lived on my Social Security check, and played out my days as the victim. You know, "Poor J. He was never the same after Jackson left. I'm sure that death came as a relief to him." No, don't think so. But symbolically, I died in June 1999, in Gardner, Massachusetts, along with my beliefs, and yes, Jude Barnes stepped in and took a "lease". You do what you need to do to survive. It was simple, really. I chose to flip the coin and see it as being to my advantage. It seemed to be the only way that I could get my arms around this obstacle in my life, this deceit that so overwhelmed me. And, the finished product is what you have before you, at least in writing. Sure, there are plenty of things still to change; physically, I'm still a wreck from the surgeries, and the aftermath of 11 years of chronic illness and the post-traumatic condition of my liver is still playing havoc with my well-being, at times. It would also be great if the day ever came that I could actually balance my checkbook. That would be a significant change and probably make my bank very happy. However, now when people ask, I don't tell them that Jackson left me, I tell them that he **set me free**. Just flip that coin and make it to your advantage. However, I must also give my mother her credit in this. I realized that she was right about something. When she told me that once she knew the truth about my father, she couldn't take him back, I didn't see the real meaning of that statement. I do now, though. Once you know how someone actually feels about you, it makes all the difference in the world. But, whereas my mother chose to be defeated by her truth, I realized that I had to deal with it and move on. So, thanks Mom. I owe you one…

As for this little side-trip in my life, now may it rest in peace and bother me no more. I have stopped, looked, AND listened. It was worth every moment of the past six years' existence that I have lived to know what I now know about life, about my place in life, about my values and how they were shaped. I am living because I deserve to live. I think as well that I finally grew up. As my doctor said when he told me that I was going to live, "Now for the bad news. You have to get a life." I am more than ready.

Chapter Eighteen

**"And, if it isn't in your own back yard, you
never really lost it, to begin with."
Judy Garland, "The Wizard of Oz"**

M y landlord and I have our morning ritual of drinking our
coffee while sitting in the garden, discussing our day, our
lives, our world.

The other day we were talking and he commented on how
his wisteria vine had not bloomed for three-four years and he
wondered what was wrong; I had to admit that it was a huge vine,
covering most of his deck. Whatever is in this soil, it works.

So, I told him to ask St. Jude for help; however, he told
me that he was not comfortable dealing with St. Jude because you
had to re-pay him for answered prayers. A voice told me to go to
the vine. I stood up and walked over to it and placed both hands
on its trunk and I prayed, "Dear St. Jude, give him one flower so
he will believe that you exist." I sat down and we continued our
talk. That was Thursday afternoon. I thought nothing more about
it. The following Sunday, I had been doing some errands and
came home. When I pulled into the driveway, my landlord was
there. "Come here. I have something to show you." I thought,
"Oh, God. What has Marilyn done?" Marilyn's my buddy, my
cat. Down the path went my landlord with me following, looking

for damage. He stopped at the cottage and turned around, pointing to the deck. "Look!" I turned and looked. Just above where I had held on to the trunk, on top of all the green leaves, there stood one beautiful purple flower. I was ecstatic! I ran up the steps of the deck for a closer look; I was yelling for joy; I ran around the yard and hugged my landlord. "Stop that! Calm down!" I yelled, "Look! St. Jude answered my prayer! He gave you a flower!" I have had several moments in my life where I have felt the presence of God. Because of these, I know in my bones that He exists within each of us. And I say without hesitation that St. Jude came to this garden and touched that vine. I was telling someone this story at work the other day and teasingly, she said, "It's the simple things in life that satisfy you, Jude." So they are, but I reminded her that it is the simple things that become the monumental moments in one's life; falling in love, marrying, the blessing of children, the death of parents, etc. These are all every-day matters in everyone's life, but are all major turning points in our paths.

I recently saw a photo of Jackson and his new partner. The other important fact, and the reason why I wanted to see a photo of him, was I knew it would tell me if he was happy, or not. In that photo, Jackson is not happy. He's got that forced smile on his face. But, when you look at his eyes...they're dead. I know that look very well, having seen it many, many times over the 10+ years we were together. That is not the face of a happy man. I don't want to get beyond this. It has motivated me for years to keep on living, hoping that I would see him again, once more. The only way I can hope to make you understand is for you to entrust your heart to someone you love and then have them tell you that they have been waiting for you to die so they can get on with living their life. Then, I want you to sit in an empty room in an empty house, having watched everything that you created and collected for 10+ years thinking you're making a life together, all being carried out the door to a place and a life being created without you.

We all want to know if our ex's are happy, or not. Looking at that photo, I would say that Jackson has finally discovered that money cannot buy everything. He always claimed that it was difficult for him to look me in the eyes when he had something to tell me, because I made him feel as if I was looking right through him to his soul. He was right, and I can still do it, thousands of miles and years away from him. Seeing that photo was an answered prayer.

I'll make a promise to all of you...before I die, I will see that man again and when that moment comes, we will be on equal ground; face to face, eye to eye.

Folks, with your guts on the floor next to your barely-beating heart, look to God. What other choice is left to us? Suicide? No, thank you. Having tried it as a teenager, I realized that suicide is too permanent an answer. What if you're wrong? Seriously, of the traumas I have experienced and survived, why on earth would I have contemplated suicide?

But before I go, I want you to know about my friend, Cassie. I met Cassie the very day I moved to Rochester in 1985. We instantly bonded, both being Italian, etc. I saw Cassie through her two pregnancies, going to nursing school, her affair, her divorce; everything. I would tell her that she was the sister I had always wanted. I'd go to her house, she would come to ours, and we'd yak for hours with her kids running around having a ball. As well, Cassie came to Massachusetts to help me with my mother when she was so ill. She loved that my mother had been a nurse for so many years. As it turned out, when I moved back to Rochester after our breakup, I found Cassie a second job working for the same company where I worked and our friendship continued, as it always had.

And, it was Cassie who betrayed me to Jackson. She was the one Nelson had warned me of, only he never gave me her name. I often wonder if he knew it was going to be Cassie. Apparently, after our breakup, she remained friends with Jackson and never told me. She would talk with him regularly and he would send her tickets to fly to New York City to meet him when he was there on a shopping spree, to keep him company. On and on it went. One day while we were talking on the phone, I asked her if she ever heard from him. Something was bugging me since I had come back to Rochester about Cassie and wouldn't let go until I asked her. That psychic thing of mine. She admitted to everything. She told me that she had maintained a friendship with Jackson and that he would send for her to meet him, etc. She also told me that whenever they spoke, I was the first thing he would ask her about. "How's J.? Have you heard from him? Where is he? What is he doing?" I was so stunned, I had to sit down. Cassie. My closest friend. I didn't mind that she had maintained a friendship with Jackson. That was her business. But, I never once asked her anything about him, although I suspected something was up. I never asked until that day and I learned of her betrayal. I never spoke to her again. I immediately e-mailed Jackson at his office, telling him what I had discovered and what a coward I thought he was; to do it through someone I considered a friend, instead of asking me. My betrayal. Again, Nelson was right about it all.

Regarding Jackson, my mother and my family, now they are all in their proper places in my life.

If anything ever should come of this story, my only hope and prayer to dear St. Jude is that it helps someone else, as well. Re-living it has certainly helped me. Share your experiences...you could help someone. You could help yourself.

As for my feelings for Jackson. Yes, there are still feelings there, can't deny that and don't want to, either. When something so life-changing as this happens to a person, I can only say that you must take responsibility in some form for the act because you orchestrated it, not the other person. We all live the life we create. Had I not let Jackson back into my life, had I listened to my inner voice telling me to run, none of this would have taken place. And, the other aspect that I can take responsibility for...my feelings for Jackson. I can't help how he feels about me. That is beyond my control. However, I can accept the fact that I was in love with him and recognize those feelings within myself. There is nothing wrong with doing that. What I chose to ignore during those years we were together was my own doing, not his. So yes, the feelings are there and I acknowledge their existence because they show me that I have the ability to love AND to forgive. My stupidity was in how often I chose to forgive.

Making so many changes in my life doesn't erase any part of my experience or time spent with Jackson. It does however finally close the door on that chapter of my life and only I carry the key to that door. Why? Because I take responsibility for what took place in my life during that time which means that I take control of that period in my life, it no longer controls me. Does it work? There have been days when all I can ponder is why it all happened. Why was I given back my life at a time when it meant absolutely nothing to me? Maybe it was to show me that my life has got to have meaning for me, before it can matter a damn to anyone else. The one mistake I did not make was in jumping right into another relationship. I can't tell you how many times I have seen that happen, only for my friends or family members to experience exactly what they previously endured. No, thanks. I prefer pulling off the road and checking for damages and why they happened. Fix it. It's broken; the broken part being you. Don't wonder why people always treat you a certain way or why a certain type is always attracted to you. The one thing in thoughts of this nature that remains the same is you, which is very odd because it is the one thing you can change which then will change the entire landscape of your life. I've said it before...growing up is a bitch, especially at 50. A great saying that I repeat in my mind almost daily is, "If it ain't your responsibility, don't comment." What a hush that would bring to a crowd, ainna? Time to sweep our own front steps. The final positive point I have discovered, and probably the most important, is to get involved in something bigger than yourself and your life if you ever want to regain control of your life and get over something. You have got to get out of it and look at it and find something bigger in which to become involved. Then, go back in and work on you.

This story is my reward for facing my demons –
the luxury of a simple and uncomplicated life

I have my friends, my cottage, my cat and my beloved
"Secret Garden"

I continue to explore the astonishment of living and finally,
as we say in Italian, basta; it really is
"enough"

FINIS

CURTAIN

THE END

COME ON, TURN THE PAGE...

IS IT?

www.ingramcontent.com/pod-product-compliance
Lightning Source LLC
Chambersburg PA
CBHW051137020726
47501CB00005B/1543